"Will you think over my offer?"

Sabrina hesitated. Everything inside her screamed yes, but rational thought threw in a note of caution and reality. "I... Oh, Marc."

He stared down at her. "Just forget the other man in your life." There was a grim note to his voice now.

"If only it were that simple," she said sadly.

KATHRYN ROSS was born in Zambia, Africa, where her parents happened to live at that time. Educated in Ireland and England, she now lives in a village near Blackpool, Lancashire. Kathryn is a professional beauty therapist, but writing is her first love. As a child she wrote adventure stories, and at thirteen was editor of her school magazine. Happily, ten writing years later, *Designed With Love* was accepted by Harlequin. A romantic Sagittarian, she loves traveling to exotic locations.

Books by Kathryn Ross

KATHRYN ROSS

Whisper of Scandal

Harlequin Books

TORONTO • NEW YORK • LONDON
AMSTERDAM • PARIS • SYDNEY • HAMBURG
STOCKHOLM • ATHENS • TOKYO • MILAN
MADRID • WARSAW • BUDAPEST • AUCKLAND

ISBN 0-373-11898-8

WHISPER OF SCANDAL

First North American Publication 1997.

Copyright © 1994 by Kathryn Ross.

All rights reserved. Except for use in any review, the reproduction or utilization of this work in whole or in part in any form by any electronic, mechanical or other means, now known or hereafter invented, including xerography, photocopying and recording, or in any information storage or retrieval system, is forbidden without the written permission of the publisher, Harlequin Enterprises Limited, 225 Duncan Mill Road, Don Mills, Ontario, Canada M3B 3K9.

All characters in this book have no existence outside the imagination of the author and have no relation whatsoever to anyone bearing the same name or names. They are not even distantly inspired by any individual known or unknown to the author, and all incidents are pure invention.

This edition published by arrangement with Harlequin Books S.A.

® and TM are trademarks of the publisher. Trademarks indicated with ® are registered in the United States Patent and Trademark Office, the Canadian Trade Marks Office and in other countries.

Printed in U.S.A.

CHAPTER ONE

'WE SHOULDN'T really be doing this,' Sabrina told Garth nervously.

'Why ever not?' He leaned across and poured her some more wine. 'I think that bringing you out for dinner was a lovely idea.'

'Yes, but, Garth, we have got to be sensible.' Her eyes flickered over the intimate booths lit by candlelight, searching for any face that she might recognise. This was one of London's most expensive restaurants and it was a well-known haunt of many famous people... including MPs like Garth Fraiser. It was not the type of place to have a secret meeting. 'I'm sure you don't usually bring your ex-secretaries to places like this.'

'Well, you are not the usual kind of secretary,' Garth answered with a smile.

Bright blue eyes swung back on to his attractive face. Despite his advancing years Garth Fraiser was still a good-looking man. His strawberry-blond hair was thick and vital, the deep lines on his face emphasising his strong, stubborn character.

'Exactly.' She said the word quietly but with meaning. 'And we don't want to start people talking.'

'I'm sorry, Sabrina... I don't want to place you in an awkward position.' He sighed and leaned back in his chair. 'You've been through so much recently... what with the death of your mother and... everything. It's

5

just that we need to talk; I have so much to explain to you.'

For a moment her blue eyes clouded with sadness. 'I know,' she said softly. 'But it's you I'm worried about. What would your wife say if she knew that you were out having dinner with me?'

He smiled. 'She would think it was business. Anyway, Nadine is in Paris visiting Marc. She won't be back until tomorrow.'

'Are you going to tell her?' Sabrina's beautiful face was etched with strain as she waited for his answer.

'I don't think I could face it.' Garth shrugged helplessly. 'I do care about you, Sabrina. I know you must find that hard to believe. I've made a lot of mistakes. The main one being that I should have told Nadine years ago.' He raked a hand through his hair in agitation. 'Look, come back to work for me, Brina, and we'll work things out. I miss you.'

'Thank you, Garth.' She swallowed down a sudden lump of emotion in her throat. 'I miss you too.' She did miss him; she also missed the cut and thrust of political life at the Palace of Westminster. 'But having me as your secretary could cause you problems.' She forced herself to be practical. 'Politics is your life and, as you have said yourself, people expect you to be whiter than white. If word got out about me it could bring you down . . . it could certainly go against your moving to Brussels next year.'

He sighed. 'I certainly don't want to risk ruining my political career. This job as Euro MP next year means a hell of a lot to me.'

She nodded. 'You've worked very hard for the posting.'

'I suppose I have...' He paused thoughtfully. 'So has Nadine. She has always been wonderfully supportive.'

Sabrina nodded her head. She had met Garth's wife on a few occasions. Nadine was French, extremely beautiful and very intelligent. People liked and respected her and she was certainly an asset to Garth's career. 'But she is not stupid, Garth. It's only a matter of time before she notices something is amiss. I don't want to pressurise you, but I think you should either tell her or cut me out of your life altogether.'

Although she said the words firmly, there was a tremor inside her body. She hated the thought of losing Garth out of her life... especially now, in the light of what she had found out. She wanted to get to know him better, to talk things through... to deepen their relationship.

'Surely you don't mean that?' He frowned and for a moment his face turned pale as he reached across the table to catch her hand.

Her eyes clouded and she shook her head. 'No... no, of course I don't. I was just trying to be sensible.'

'I can't tell Nadine, Brina. I——'

A dark shadow fell over the table, startling them out of their engrossing conversation.

'And just what is it that you can't tell Nadine?' a deep voice enquired in crisp tones.

Sabrina had to tip her head back to look up at the man who was staring down at them. Her hand left Garth's with guilty haste as her eyes locked with a burning dark gaze.

'Marc, this is a surprise!' Garth rose quickly to his feet, for once looking completely disconcerted. 'Is Nadine with you?'

'No. Mother is still in France.'

'I see.' Garth smiled and seemed to regain his composure on hearing that his wife was not about to appear beside them. 'I'm dining with my secretary, Miss Sabrina Harrington.' He waved a hand towards her and the man turned his gaze down on her again. 'This is my stepson Marc Kingsley.'

Sabrina's one overriding thought as she looked up at him was that Marc Kingsley was far, far too good-looking.

Dark hair and eyes and a tanned skin made him look more French than English, but his weren't the conventional good looks. There was something hard and forceful about that face that stared down at her. For a moment she thought she saw a flicker of surprise in the intense black eyes as they lingered on her long strawberry-blonde hair and heart-shaped face. The way he looked at her was so openly arrogant that it made her flush uncomfortably.

'Miss Harrington.' He acknowledged her with a brief nod of his head before turning back to Garth. 'I called at the house and your housekeeper told me that I might find you here.'

Garth nodded. 'Yes, I left the number in case Nadine phoned.' He indicated the spare seat next to them. 'Won't you join us, Marc?'

'For a few minutes.' With a brief glance at his gold wristwatch he sat down directly facing Sabrina. 'I just wanted to tell you that Mother has changed her plans and won't be coming back until after the weekend. She decided to fly down to Nice for a couple of days to see her sister.'

'Oh...' Garth frowned. 'There is nothing wrong, is there?'

'No, no. Just a spur-of-the-moment whim,' Marc assured him swiftly.

'Well, I'm glad you told me. I was going to ring her at your home in Paris tonight. I would have been concerned if there had been no answer.'

'Well, as usual she is staying at the Sheldon in Nice. Why don't you ring her now, Garth? I'm sure she will be having an early night tonight. She left Paris early this morning but, knowing my mother, she will have been into every boutique in Nice by now.'

'Yes, and probably bought them out.' Garth grinned and turned his attention to Sabrina. 'Will you excuse me for a moment while I go and ring my wife?' he asked with his usual gentle courtesy.

Before she had time to open her mouth, however, Marc Kingsley was answering for her. 'Of course she will— I'm sure that Miss Harrington wouldn't dream of standing in the way of true love.' Although his voice was light, the eyes that met hers across the table were deep and somehow disturbing in their intensity.

Why did she feel that answering that statement could be decidedly dangerous? It was merely a light-hearted jesting comment...wasn't it?

Garth obviously thought that it was, because he was smiling down at her as he got to his feet. 'I won't be long; don't let my stepson charm you too much while I'm away.'

Sabrina for some reason felt a little embarrassed by that comment. She gave Marc a polite smile that was a trifle nervous.

He didn't return the gesture, just continued to look across at her with unfathomable eyes.

'So, Miss Harrington, is this a working dinner or a more pleasurable interlude?' he asked in a low tone.

Was it her imagination or was there a cutting edge in his voice? She toyed with the glass in front of her with long nervous fingers. Although Garth had introduced her as his secretary, in point of fact she no longer worked for him. She contemplated telling Marc Kingsley that, then changed her mind. It would be far safer just to go along with what Garth had said. 'Just a working dinner,' she said lightly.

'Really?' There it was again, an almost sarcastic edge in the velvety deep voice. Candlelight flickered over the strong, handsome features without lending any softness to the harsh, remote countenance. 'How long have you been working for my stepfather, Miss Harrington?'

She hesitated. 'About a year.' She felt as if she was being interrogated, and shifted restlessly in her chair.

'I see.' He met her eyes directly. 'And where do you work now?'

The blunt question made Sabrina's nerves flutter. 'Now?' She looked at him with wide blue eyes, her brain seizing up with panic.

'Now that you no longer work for Garth,' he said easily.

Their eyes met and held. He had known all along that she was no longer Garth's secretary!

He smiled, showing even white teeth. 'My mother let it slip that Garth was looking for a new secretary and that you were very hard to replace.'

'Oh...I see.' She struggled to gather her thoughts together. She felt for one moment like a frightened little mouse trapped in a corner by a large cat. 'Well, I haven't got another job yet.' She kept her voice cool with a great effort of will. 'So I still do a bit of work for Garth at home...just odd bits of typing really.'

'I see,' he drawled with a smile. 'Lucky Garth. I wish I had someone like you. Someone I could call on for the odd bit of typing.'

There was something about the almost sardonic note of his voice that sent shivers of alarm racing through her. Was he casting some kind of nasty suspicion on her relationship with Garth?

She looked across at him with a frown, and he smiled. It was a pleasant enough smile. Maybe she was just paranoid, she told herself crisply. She felt uncomfortable dining here with Garth and because of that she was reading things into this man's words—things that probably didn't exist.

'I am very highly qualified and there are some things that Garth likes me to take care of personally for him,' she emphasised crisply. 'Just until he gets a new permanent secretary.'

'Oh, I'm sure that you have all the necessary qualifications.' For a brief second his eyes moved away from her creamy complexion and down the slender column of her neck to where the top buttons of her jade silk blouse were undone.

'And you are very easy on the eye...a definite bonus,' he drawled lazily.

She could feel her sensitive skin prickling with the heat of embarrassment. She didn't know what to say to that.

He smiled, his gaze moving over the peach glow on her high cheekbones to lock with her eyes. 'Yes, very beautiful...sensuously so.' The dark eyes moved to the softness of her mouth, a feature that she had always considered a little too full for her liking. 'On the whole,

Sabrina Harrington, I would say that you are one dangerous package.'

The air between them was charged with tension and some strange emotion that Sabrina could not define. She tried to steady her erratic breathing so that she could make some kind of a reply to his outrageous comments, but with those dark eyes boring into her she found it impossible.

Garth's return caught her by surprise but seemingly not Marc, for he turned with an easy smile towards his stepfather as he took his seat beside him. 'Well, did you manage to get through to Mother?'

'Yes, I did.' There was a heaviness in Garth's voice that brought Sabrina's attention winging sharply back towards him. His skin had a grey tinge to it, and the lines around his eyes were more deeply etched.

'Is everything all right?' she asked in sudden concern.

'Yes, I'm just feeling a little tired. If you are finished, Brina, I think I would like to leave.'

'Yes, of course.' In her agitation she didn't notice that he had slipped into using his pet name for her, something they had agreed not to do. In public they had agreed to keep things strictly formal. She bent to pick up her handbag, anxious to get away from the intimidating stranger opposite and find out the real reason why Garth was suddenly looking so ill.

'Seeing that you are tired, Garth, why don't I run your secretary home for you?'

The casually proffered suggestion had Sabrina straightening very quickly, a refusal forming on her lips. She would rather take a taxi than ride with Marc Kingsley. He made her feel so on edge it was untrue.

'Would you mind, Marc? I would be very grateful,' Garth got in ahead of her, however.

'Not at all; it will be my pleasure.' Dark eyes gleamed as he noticed that she was not exactly overjoyed by the situation. 'Stay where you are and I will go and ask the doorman to bring the cars around for us. Have you got your keys?'

As soon as Marc had moved away from them Sabrina leaned across towards Garth. 'What on earth is the matter?' she asked nervously.

'Nothing, sweetheart.' His voice strove to reassure her but the worried light refused to die away from her eyes. He sighed. 'Nadine and I just had a slight argument. It was nothing much but I hate to upset her like that.'

'What was it all about?'

He hesitated for a moment. 'She wants me to fly out to Nice tomorrow and spend the weekend there with her. I told her I couldn't come.'

'Why ever not?' She frowned at him. 'It's Saturday tomorrow and you told me yourself that you have nothing very much on.'

'Yes, I have, Brina. I wanted to see you tomorrow...we have so much to discuss.'

'No, Garth.' Sabrina's voice was adamant. 'You must put your wife first——'

'I'm not prepared to argue about this,' Garth cut across her. 'I'm spending tomorrow with you and there is an end to it. I thought that we could drive into the country——'

'No,' she interrupted his plans firmly.

'Good, that's settled, then,' Garth continued smoothly as if she hadn't spoken. 'I'll pick you up at ten.' He rose to his feet and smiled down at her.

'You are incorrigible,' she said on a note of dry humour.

'But you love me anyway?' He winked down at her.

'You know I do,' she answered huskily.

For a moment his eyes lingered on her. 'Thank you, Brina. You don't know how happy that makes me.' He hesitated and seemed about to say more, then glanced over as his stepson started to walk back across the restaurant towards them. 'Brina, do me a favour, will you?' he asked quickly.

'If it is within my power, you know I will.'

'Don't let anything slip to Marc about us. I'd hate Nadine to find out like that.'

'You know I wouldn't say anything,' she reassured him quickly.

Garth nodded. 'Marc is a very shrewd man. Also a very charming one. Just be careful, Brina.'

'Well, I'm not easily charmed.' Sabrina smiled. 'Now, will you go to Nice tomorrow and see your wife?'

He shook his head. 'I will be seeing you tomorrow. Ten o'clock sharp.' He moved away then before she had time to argue the point further.

She watched him go with a mixture of impatience and affection. He had to be the most pigheaded, stubborn man that she had ever come across. He had probably accepted Marc's offer to run her home just so that she didn't get the chance to try and change his mind.

She watched him stop and talk with his stepson on the way out of the door. She had always thought that Garth was a powerfully built man, yet next to Marc Kingsley's lean, broad-shouldered frame he looked almost small.

For a moment she racked her brain to remember any information that Garth had given her on his stepson.

He was a successful man, a wealthy industrialist who spent most of his time in Paris but also had a home in Surrey. She knew that his mother Nadine was French and that his father had been English. They were the only facts that she could call to mind. With a sigh she got to her feet and went over to join them. Somehow she had the feeling that she needed to know much more about Marc Kingsley in order to step very warily around him.

Did he have to watch her like that? she wondered angrily as she moved nearer to them. His eyes were raking over her slim figure in the pencil-straight skirt and jade blouse as if he were assessing how much she would fetch on the open market.

'Ready?' he asked abruptly as she reached his side.

She nodded, not trusting herself to speak. It was very strange, but this man seemed capable of stirring up her temper without even saying anything. Just one look from those eyes seemed to increase her temperature rapidly.

The darkness outside was a relief. It was a few minutes' respite from Marc Kingsley's probing eyes, a few minutes to compose herself. A bright red Porsche drew up beside them and the car-park attendant got out and handed Marc the keys.

Her eyes ran disdainfully over the sleek lines of the red Porsche. Nothing subdued for Mr Kingsley, she thought wryly. His taste in women was probably the same as his taste in cars. He would like them flashy and elegant.

He surprised her by opening the passenger door for her before going around to the other side. At least the man had some manners.

She frowned. What on earth was the matter with her? It wasn't like her to be so aggressive, especially towards a perfect stranger. The man was doing her a favour by taking her home and here she was tearing him to shreds. In fact ever since he had first looked down at her she had been on the defensive—it was most unlike her.

She watched him as he secured his seatbelt and then started the powerful engine. His face was lit for a moment by the street-light as he turned towards her. It looked all planes and angles in the half-light, emphasising just how ruggedly attractive he was. For a crazy second her heart seemed to dip downwards and thud like a sledge-hammer against her chest.

'Aren't you going to put on your seatbelt?' he enquired lazily.

'Oh...yes.' For some reason her fingers felt like thumbs as she struggled awkwardly with the belt.

'Here, let me do it.' He leaned across and took it from her hands with a brisk impatient movement. Inadvertently his fingers brushed against the silk of her blouse as he pulled it across her, the soft touch sending a million sensory nerve-endings throbbing into life.

'There.' The belt slotted firmly into place and he was swinging the car out into the stream of traffic, the large hands looking strong and capable on the wheel.

Sabrina swallowed hard and looked away from him out through the window. She felt confused and angry with herself. She was twenty-five years of age and had been out with plenty of men in the past, but none of them had made her body respond the way it had done just now from a mere casual contact. Marc Kingsley was having a very strange effect on her. She was undeniably attracted to him, just as every woman who ever came into contact with him would probably be. But there was something else. He inflamed her senses. Angered her, excited her, frightened her. She couldn't understand how a total stranger could arouse such emotions.

She tried to switch her thoughts away from him as they drove down busy roads through the heart of London. It was a magical city at night, she thought idly, with all the beautiful buildings illuminated by a warm orange glow against the velvet darkness of the sky.

Marc was pulling up outside her apartment in Kensington before she realised that he had driven her straight to her door without having to ask where she lived.

She turned to him with a frown. 'How did you know my address?'

'Garth told me before he left.'

'Oh, I see.'

Marc turned off the engine and the sudden silence seemed heavy and oppressive. The only sound that filled Sabrina's ears was the wild thud of her heartbeats.

'Well, thank you for the lift home,' she said a trifle breathlessly, reaching for the door-handle.

'Aren't you going to invite me in for coffee?' he asked silkily.

She hesitated, taken back by the request. 'Well, I...yes—yes, of course.' Hell, she was babbling like a teenager. What on earth was wrong with her?

He stood behind her as she opened her front door and she was annoyed to find that her hand shook as she tried to get the key in the lock.

'Do you need some help?'

His drily amused voice flustered her even more.

'No, thank you.' Thankfully the door swung open and Sabrina led the way into the elegant hallway.

The apartment was very large and decorated in a stylishly modern way. Crystal lights illuminated warm peach walls and highlighted the thick beige carpet that ran through each room.

'Nice apartment,' Marc remarked as his eyes moved over the lounge with its large cream leather suite and the modern pictures that lent vibrant splashes of colour to the room. 'Working for Garth must pay well.'

Sabrina's eyebrow lifted at such a remark. Really, who did the man think he was? It was none of his business where her money came from.

She decided not to answer such a remark but instead waved him towards the settee. 'Make yourself comfortable,' she said stiffly. 'I'll just put the kettle on.'

Instead of going into the lounge, however, he followed her into the kitchen.

She flicked a disgruntled glance at him as he leaned nonchalantly against the marble worktops to watch her fill the kettle.

'The view's better in here,' he drawled lazily as he caught her eye, and then his gaze moved slowly from her neat ankles up over her long legs and curving body.

She felt her body heat start to rise at that look, and she turned away impatiently to open the cupboards and get out some china cups and saucers. Why did he keep looking at her like that?

'So why did you give up working for my stepfather, Sabrina?' he asked casually.

Her fingers slipped on the bone-china cup she had been reaching for and she watched in horror as it fell with a crashing sound on to the tiled floor. 'Damn!' Her dismayed voice sounded loud in the silence.

He bent to help her pick up the pieces. 'Shame,' he murmured as he turned the end of the cup over. 'Royal Doulton as well—a very expensive piece.'

She glared at him. 'What are you anyway, a tax inspector?' she asked stiffly. 'You've done nothing but make references to how expensive things are.'

He looked at her with raised eyebrows. 'Have I? I'm sorry...things of beauty just fascinate me.' As he spoke his eyes moved over her face searchingly.

She bit down heavily on her lower lip and her blue eyes clouded with tears. 'No...*I'm* sorry.' She got up quickly and went to wrap the slivers of china in paper before putting them in the bin. 'I shouldn't have snapped at you like that. It's just...well, that tea service had sentimental memories. It was my mother's.' She didn't turn to face him as she spoke—she was desperately trying to collect her emotions. It was so silly to be upset about something as small as a teacup, but it had brought thoughts of her mother vividly to her mind.

'You'll have to forgive me.' She forced a smile to her lips and turned to face him. 'My mother died a couple of months ago and I'm not fully myself yet.'

'That's understandable.' His voice was surprisingly gentle, his eyes sympathetic now as they lingered on her bright, shimmering eyes. 'Why don't I make the coffee?' he suggested with a smile. 'You sit down for a moment.'

'No...really.' She tried to protest but he had already drawn out one of the kitchen chairs for her and was busy getting more cups out of the cupboard. It seemed futile to argue so she sat and watched him.

It seemed very strange to have such an attractive man in her kitchen making her coffee. He looked very out of place in the pretty kitchen. He was so suave and debonair in the immaculately cut suit, and yet so very masculine. Marc Kingsley just seemed to ooze sex appeal.

'Do you take milk and sugar?' he asked, interrupting her thoughts and making her jump.

'No.' She shook her head.

'We have something in common.' He smiled warmly at her as he placed the coffee in front of her.

They had more than he knew in common, she thought suddenly. 'Would you prefer to sit in the lounge? It's more comfortable,' she said as he sat down opposite her.

'No, I'm fine.' He stretched out his long legs and reached for his cup. His hands looked very large against the delicate china, she noticed absently.

'Well, I must say that I'm very glad that I decided to go in search of Garth tonight,' he said suddenly.

She looked up at him with questioning eyes.

'Otherwise we might never have met,' he enlightened her softly.

She tried to will herself not to blush at that remark and laughed. 'Garth told me to beware of your famous charm.'

'Did he now?' For just a second there was that undercurrent of steel in his tone again. Then he smiled. 'Well, you have the advantage. He has never mentioned you to me.'

She sipped her coffee. 'Well, when you are a private secretary you tend to learn a few things about your boss's family now and then,' she said lightly.

'I suppose you do.' He put his cup down. 'You were about to tell me why you stopped working for Garth.'

'Was I?' She frowned for a moment. 'You know, you really ask a lot of questions, Mr Kingsley.' She held his gaze for a moment.

'That's because I'm very interested in you,' he drawled huskily. 'And the name's Marc.'

Sabrina's blood-pressure seemed to roar in her ears at that. 'I'm flattered.' Was Marc Kingsley really interested in her? Sabrina's heart thudded wildly at the thought. 'I'm flattered,' she said again, trying very hard to keep a coolness in her voice. She was completely at a loss for what to say next.

'Good.' He smiled. 'So how about having lunch with me tomorrow?'

The question was so smoothly asked that it took Sabrina's mind a moment to assimilate it. Marc Kingsley was asking her for a date! For one wild moment she was tempted to say yes. Then she remembered Garth. For his sake it would be prudent to keep her distance from Marc Kingsley; the connection was too close. Anyway, Garth was taking her out tomorrow.

'I'm sorry——' she shook her head regretfully '—but I can't.'

'Am I stepping on someone else's toes?' he asked, his gaze never wavering from the bright blue of her eyes.

'Well...' She hesitated, unsure which was the best way to get out of this. If she said no, Marc might just suggest another date; if she said yes, he might ask her who her boyfriend was. 'I have a date tomorrow,' she said at last.

'So how about the day after?' he persisted.

She shook her head. 'I...I can't, Marc. I'm involved with someone else and it wouldn't be fair.'

'Lucky man,' he drawled softly. 'Well——' he finished his coffee and stood up '—I suppose I should be going.'

She suppressed the immediate feeling of disappointment. Given different circumstances she would have loved to see this man again. There was something about him that was quite fascinating. 'Thank you for the lift,' she said politely as she stood up to walk with him to the door.

He smiled. Then quite suddenly he reached across and touched her face. 'You know, I never take no for an answer...it goes against the grain.'

'Don't you?' Her voice sounded as breathless as she felt.

'Certainly not.' His finger trailed softly across the smooth skin of her cheekbone. 'I'll be seeing you soon, Sabrina Harrington,' he promised decisively.

She watched him walk away from her with a pounding heart. Her skin seemed to burn where he had touched her. For one wild moment she was ecstatic that he would ask her out again. Then as he closed the front door behind him reality set in.

She couldn't get involved with Marc Kingsley. It would be sheer folly. She turned to clear the table and then turned out the lights with a sigh. What would Marc think if he knew the truth? she wondered suddenly. Would he still be so keen to pursue her if he knew she was Garth Fraiser's illegitimate daughter? The question taunted her as she made her way to her bedroom. Of course she would never have an answer; that was a secret she had to guard very close to her heart.

CHAPTER TWO

GARTH collected Sabrina promptly at ten the next morning and they drove out to the countryside in his Aston Martin.

It was a beautiful day. Sunshine played over the fresh green of the fields. The trees were knotted with buds ready to burst forward at any time and daffodils brightened the verges of the road.

Sabrina felt her spirits lift. Winter had been particularly grim for her and the promise of warmer, brighter days ahead was wonderful. It was like coming out of a long, dark tunnel into golden light.

She turned to Garth with a smile. 'So where are we going? You're being very mysterious.'

'Well...' He hesitated. 'I thought it would be a good idea to bring you out to my house for lunch.'

'Oh!' She frowned. Somehow it didn't seem right to go to his home, not when Nadine knew nothing about her; it seemed devious somehow. 'What about your housekeeper? Won't she think it's funny that I'm having lunch with you?'

'Don't worry about Sadie; she'll just think that you are coming to take notes. I've told her I'm having a working lunch.' He smiled reassuringly at her. 'I've decided we need to have a good heart-to-heart talk and the only place we won't be interrupted is in my study.'

He was probably right. They did need to talk. It had been a hell of a shock to find out that Garth Fraiser was

her father, especially when her mother had led her to
believe that her father was dead. She still found it hard
to comprehend.

She had spotted the advertisement for the job as
Garth's private secretary in a newspaper—or rather her
mother had drawn her attention to it. It had been ideal,
exactly what she had been looking for, and she had gone
for an interview with high hopes. She'd known her
qualifications were good and so were her references, but
she'd also known that competition for the job would be
stiff. She had been ecstatic when she'd got the job.

Working for Garth had been exhausting at times but
she had enjoyed every moment of it. He had worked her
hard but he had always been fair with her and she had
respected him greatly.

Then just a few months ago when her mother had
died in a tragic motorway accident, leaving Sabrina devastated, Garth had been wonderful. He had given her
as much time off as she needed in order to sort things
out. He had been kind and sympathetic and had even
offered to help her with the arrangements for the fu-
neral. At the time she had thought it was exceptionally
kind of him, and she had been touched by his gener-
osity, but she had never for one moment suspected the
truth.

It had been two weeks after Lucy Harrington's death
that she'd discovered her diaries. It was then that she'd
discovered that her mother had known Garth Fraiser
years ago. That the two had in fact attended the same
university and later they had both worked in the same
law firm before Garth had got involved in politics. This
had puzzled her intensely. Why hadn't her mother mentioned that she knew her boss? Why the secrecy?

She had sat down to read the rest of the diaries with avid curiosity. What she had discovered had changed her whole life and she had been angry, bitterly angry that her mother had lied to her, that Garth had deceived her. Had he only given her the job as his secretary because of who she was? That question had haunted and humiliated her, and her first move had been to quit her job and to tell Garth Fraiser exactly what she thought of him.

Now her anger and her shock had cooled and she could feel sorrow at the situation, sympathy for her mother and for Garth. Lord, it was all such a mess. She pushed a hand through her hair in a distraught gesture. If only her mother had told her the truth... if only.

'Damn!' Garth pulled the car to a standstill at the gateway to a large Victorian house.

'What is it?' Sabrina's gaze darted from her father to the house in front of them. Even as she asked the question she noticed the bright red Porsche parked on the gravel drive.

'Marc's here,' Garth answered flatly.

Sabrina's heart seemed to take up a rapid nervous tattoo immediately. 'What should we do?'

With a sigh Garth started the car forward again. 'Brazen it out,' he muttered. 'I'll tell him you've come to do some important work for me. With a bit of luck he won't stay.' He grinned at her then. 'Actually there is a stack of work you could do for me. I really miss you at the office, Brina; your replacement isn't half as efficient.'

'I'm sure you're just being kind,' Sabrina said lightly. 'But thank you.'

'No, I'm being honest,' Garth replied earnestly as he pulled up outside his front door. 'If you could see the state of my desk in there——' he nodded towards the house '—you would know what I mean.'

As they got out of the car Garth glanced across at her. 'Are you all right, Sabrina? You've gone awfully pale.'

'I'm fine.' It was a lie; she was far from fine. She had just remembered that she had told Marc she had a date this afternoon. What on earth was she going to say to him?

He was in the lounge idly flicking through a magazine, his long legs stretched out, his dark head resting against the pale gold brocade of the settee as if he had all the time in the world to kill. He stood up as they came in and his eyebrows lifted slightly as he took in Sabrina's presence. 'This is a pleasant surprise,' he drawled softly. 'I thought you had a date this afternoon, Sabrina?'

She could feel her cheeks going hotter under his intense scrutiny. 'Would you believe he had to cancel me at the last moment?' Somehow she managed to inject a humorous note into her voice. 'Some important business cropped up.' She hated lying like that; she could feel herself tensing up inside, waiting for lightning to strike her down for such a falsehood.

'I do find it rather difficult to believe, actually.' The hard words took her very much by surprise for a moment, then he softened them with a smile. 'The man obviously has no sense.'

'Well, his loss is my gain.' Garth smiled. 'Sabrina has very kindly offered to come and help me out with a bit of paperwork this afternoon.'

'Very considerate.' Marc's dark eyes never left Sabrina's face as he spoke.

'Can I get you a drink, Marc?' Garth moved towards the drinks cabinet and poured himself a whisky.

'Actually, I wouldn't mind a coffee,' Marc replied easily.

'Oh, right, I'll just go and ask Sadie.' Garth put down his drink and looked at Sabrina. 'What about you, Brina? Would you like coffee or something stronger?'

'Coffee would be nice.' Sabrina sat down on one of the comfortable two-seater settees which were at each side of the fireplace. She wished Garth wouldn't call her Brina in front of Marc... it sounded far too intimate.

They were left alone and Sabrina felt her nerves flutter apprehensively as she looked up at Garth's stepson.

He leaned a hand against the mantelpiece and stared down at her for a moment as if in deep thought. Sabrina felt that familiar tug at the bottom of her stomach. He looked magnificent, she thought abruptly. He had a wonderful physique, broad shoulders tapering to narrow hips in the well-cut grey suit. She collided with his dark eyes and looked hurriedly away from him.

'So how about dinner tonight?' he asked suddenly into the silence.

She took a deep breath. 'I can't, Marc.' It had never been so difficult to turn down a date; she desperately wanted to say yes.

'Such loyalty,' he murmured. 'You must be very serious about this man, to let him stand you up and still remain so devoted.'

She shrugged and her mind searched for some answer. The awful thing about telling lies was that it seemed to snowball; you told one small one and then others had invariably to follow. It was like painting a picture—you were never quite sure when you had finished; you could keep adding things and adding things and end up in a real muddle.

'He didn't stand me up,' she said in a dignified tone. 'He rang me and told me he couldn't make it.'

'Oh, I see.' Marc's lips curved in a cynical smile. 'Who is this paragon of virtue, anyway?'

There it was, the question she had been dreading. 'Oh, you wouldn't know him,' she said airily. 'He... he's in computers.'

'Really?' There was that tinge of sardonic humour in his voice again. Sabrina frowned, but before she had time to analyse Marc's attitude Garth came back into the room.

'Coffee will be along in a moment,' he said brightly, looking from Sabrina towards his stepson. 'So, Marc, what brings you out to see me today?'

'Actually I was rather hoping I could pick your brains about a legal matter,' Marc said easily. 'I'm in the process of buying a factory in Germany and there were a couple of things I wouldn't have minded asking your opinion on.'

'Oh?' Garth looked extremely surprised at this. 'Well, you know I'm always willing to give my considered opinion.'

'Yes, but I can see you are rather...tied up, so I won't impose on you this afternoon,' Marc said, his eyes slipping over Sabrina.

'Well, how about tomorrow?' Garth said hopefully. 'I have——'

'It will be too late tomorrow. I have a meeting on it this afternoon.' Marc shrugged. 'But don't worry about it, Garth. I'll sort it out.'

There was a moment's silence and Garth looked helplessly at Sabrina. Sabrina knew he was torn in two. Obviously he wanted to help Marc out.

'If you like, I'll make a start at clearing up that desk for you, Garth,' she said softly. 'I'm sure I'll manage on my own while you discuss this business with Marc. If I have any problems I'll come in and ask you.'

'You don't mind?' Garth asked in a dubious tone.

She shook her head.

'That's really very good of you,' Marc said smoothly.

As she glanced across at him she thought she detected a gleam of satisfaction in his dark eyes. It was almost as if he had just engineered that situation. That idea was so ludicrous that she dismissed it immediately.

'I'm really sorry about this,' Garth said in a worried tone as he showed her into his study a few minutes later.

'It's all right, Garth, really it is,' she reassured him.

'But it's not all right,' he grated impatiently. 'I wanted so much to have a few quiet moments where we could just sort ourselves out.'

'Never mind.' Sabrina glanced at his desk with a smile. 'At least I can put this into some sort of order for you.'

He grimaced as he took in the chaos that was spread over the large rosewood desk. 'I meant for you to have a relaxing afternoon,' he sighed. 'You know, I'm really surprised that Marc's asking my advice. I know I have a degree in law but he has a battery of high-powered solicitors to advise him.'

'Must be something you've had prior experience of,' Sabrina answered lightly, her mind already occupied with sorting through the correspondence on Garth's desk.

'I'll be as quick as I can,' Garth said with determination.

In the event he was nearly three hours. Garth's house-keeper brought her coffee and then a little later some light lunch. By that time Sabrina had reorganised Garth's desk for him and put his filing cabinet back in order. She was just closing it when some photographs at the far end of the room caught her attention.

She walked across to have a closer look at them. There was one of Garth with his wife Nadine and their daughter Madeline. She picked it up to have a closer look. Sabrina had never met Madeline, who had been living in the States for the last two years. Garth had often spoken about her, though, in very glowing terms. Madeline was just twenty years of age and an extremely talented artist.

Sabrina was filled with curiosity as she looked at that picture of her half-sister. After all these years of thinking she was an only child it was so strange to suddenly find out she had a sister. Not that it made any difference, she thought sadly. She would probably never get to meet Madeline.

The door opened behind her and Marc came in. 'Finished your work?' he asked drily, his eyes taking in her relaxed stance by the mantelpiece.

She frowned. It almost sounded as if he didn't believe that she had been working. 'Yes, I have actually.'

He came to stand beside her and glanced at the framed photograph in her hands. 'My half-sister Madeline,' he informed her.

He reached for another photograph. 'And this is my mother and Garth on their wedding-day.'

Sabrina glanced at the smiling, happy picture of Garth and Nadine and nodded. 'Yes, I've seen that photograph before. Garth has it on his desk at Westminster.'

'Garth's very devoted to my mother,' Marc said matter-of-factly as he put the picture down again. 'I think they are still as much in love today as they were back then.'

'Yes, they seem very happy,' she said lightly.

For a moment his gaze locked on her heart-shaped face. 'You seem very fond of Garth,' he said quietly.

She looked away from him. Sometimes there was a look in Marc's dark gaze that was deeply disturbing. 'Yes, I am. He's been very good to me.'

'Garth has a kind heart.' He paused before continuing. 'It would be very easy to play on his sympathy.'

Sabrina looked up at him with a frown. 'What's that supposed to mean?'

He smiled, then reached out a hand to tip her chin upwards so that she was forced to hold his dark gaze. 'Perhaps I'm just a little jealous? After all, you seem to spend a lot of time with Garth and I can't get so much as a lunch date out of you.'

She laughed breathlessly at that, unsure whether to take that comment seriously or not. 'That's ridiculous... I'm doing work for Garth.'

'You could always come and do some work for me.' He was standing very close to her, she noticed suddenly, her heart skipping a beat nervously. 'What do you say?' he asked huskily. 'Shall we go out for lunch tomorrow and discuss it?'

'Marc, I——' Her polite refusal was cut short abruptly as his head lowered towards hers. 'Marc,' she whispered in a helpless tone as his lips brushed against hers. The kiss was gentle at first but it sent shock-waves racing straight through Sabrina. She felt herself leaning weakly against the soft material of his jacket. Then she was kissing him back, her whole body trembling as she arched towards him, hungry for the sensuous heat spiralling through her.

He was the one to pull back from her, his hands resting on her shoulders as he looked down at her. 'Shall I pick you up at about ten o'clock?' he murmured. He sounded so cool and calm while Sabrina felt as if a time bomb had just started to tick inside her.

Confused at the way she had just responded to that kiss, Sabrina could only stare at him for a moment. 'I...I don't know.' She shook her head, trying to clear it of her muddled thoughts. 'Isn't ten o'clock a little early for lunch?'

For a brief moment there was a glimmer of triumph in his dark eyes. 'Not for what I have in mind,' he drawled softly. Then his hands left her shoulders.

She felt strangely bereft as he moved away from her. 'So ten o'clock it is,' he said decisively and Sabrina had the strange sensation of being carried along with something that was already out of control.

Garth joined them at that moment. 'There you are, Marc,' he said, looking slightly harassed. 'I'm sorry about that. Nadine has just been on the phone—she says she will be flying home tonight after all.'

'Well, that's marvellous news.' Marc smiled at Sabrina. 'Can I give you a lift back to town now that you've finished here?' he asked silkily.

'It's all right, Marc, I'll drop Sabrina back,' Garth cut in quickly. 'There are one or two things I want to discuss with her before she goes.'

Marc shrugged. 'As you wish.' For a brief moment his eyes rested on Sabrina. 'I'll see you tomorrow,' he said calmly.

Sabrina sat down for a moment as Marc left the room. Her legs felt as shaky as if she had just run a marathon.

'What was that all about?' Garth asked with a frown as his eyes moved over her pale features.

She shrugged. 'He's...he's taking me for lunch tomorrow.'

Silence met that remark and she looked up at him with anxious eyes. 'You don't mind, do you?'

'No...no.' Garth raked an unsteady hand through his hair. 'Are you serious about him, Brina?'

Sabrina gave a nervous laugh. 'I hardly know him, Garth.'

For a moment there was silence as Garth regarded her silently. 'My stepson is a good man...a bit of a womaniser. He has a tendency to break hearts——'

'Really, Garth, you don't need to worry. I can take care of myself,' she cut across him hastily, but he looked unconvinced.

'Damn it all, Sabrina...I've made such a mess of everything. I should have told my wife about you years ago. I feel I've let her down, and you and Marc——'

'Don't say that, Garth,' Sabrina interrupted him sadly. 'You haven't let anyone down. It wasn't as if you had the affair with my mother while you were married to Nadine.'

'No...but I was married when I met your mother.' He saw the look of shock on her face. 'You didn't know?'

She shook her head. 'There was nothing about that in my mother's diary.'

For a moment Garth's face was lit with a ghost of a smile. 'Dear Lucy. She hated the deceit. She felt terribly guilty.'

Sabrina could hardly take in what he was saying. She couldn't believe that her mother would have had an affair with a married man; it seemed so out of character.

The shrill ring of the phone interrupted the silence. Garth turned impatiently towards it and flicked on the answering machine. 'Let's walk out in the garden,' he suggested gently. 'At least out there we will have no interruptions.'

She nodded. She wanted to hear Garth's story...she wanted to try and place the pieces together in her mind. Maybe then she could understand why her mother had kept so many secrets from her.

Despite the sunshine it was cold outside. Garth linked his arm through hers. 'Are you warm enough, sweetheart?'

For a moment the concern in her father's voice made Sabrina's eyes mist with tears. She nodded, and he patted her hand. 'Come on; I'll give you a tour of my lovely gardens,' he said gently.

The landscape was very beautiful, and for a little while they walked in silence, just drinking in the colourful spring flowers as they both collected their thoughts.

Then Garth began his story and Sabrina forgot her surroundings as her mind closely followed his every word.

'You know, you are a lot like your mother,' he said with a sad smile. 'I thought the world of Lucy; her death was a terrible shock.'

'Yes, I miss her terribly, Garth,' she said huskily. 'We were so close...at least I thought we were close.' Her voice broke for a moment. 'I just can't understand why she didn't tell me about you. I feel as if I've been living a lie all my life.'

'Lucy did what she thought was best,' Garth said gently. 'I know she loved you very much; she never meant to hurt you.'

'Then why didn't she tell me?' Sabrina demanded, a note of anger in her tone now. 'She lied to me, Garth. She told me that my father was dead.'

'You have every right to be angry. But you have to remember that your mother was only young when she was expecting you. Attitudes to unmarried mothers have changed radically since then. In your mother's day it was very hard...' He trailed off and for a moment he seemed lost in thought. 'Lucy was such a beautiful woman...very spirited, very stubborn.' He sighed. 'She was about your age when I met her. She was an idealist—she had dreams of being a famous lawyer, a force to be reckoned with in the London courtrooms.'

'She didn't do so badly.' Sabrina smiled. Despite everything she was proud of her mother. She had been a very strong woman, a successful lawyer who had been highly respected.

'We had an affair.' Garth ran a hand through his thick hair. 'I was already married to a woman called Jessica when I met your mother.'

'Your wife didn't understand you.' Sabrina's voice for a moment was angry.

He sighed. 'I know it sounds bad, but Jessica and I were not in love. We were more or less going our different ways when I met your mother. Jessica was seeing another man, a very wealthy man whom she had set her sights on once she had discovered that I was not as lucrative a proposition as she had thought.'

'So if you loved my mother so much, why didn't you divorce your wife and marry her?' Sabrina's voice was dry.

'Oh, believe me, I would have.' He shook his head emphatically. 'But when I asked Jessica for a divorce she became hysterical. Suddenly I was the most important thing in the world. Obviously the man she had been seeing was not interested in making an honest woman of her.' His mouth twisted bitterly. 'So she figured that she would hang on to me.'

Sabrina could hear the pain in his voice and she reached out a hand to cover his. 'You don't have to tell me this,' she said suddenly. 'It doesn't matter; it's in the past now.'

'Oh, it does matter. You see, the past has a way of shaping the future.' For a moment he was silent. 'Jessica and I had a dreadful row, and I said things I shouldn't have . . . cruel things. She ran out of the apartment and straight in front of a car.'

'Oh, Garth!' Sabrina stopped and turned to look at him, shocked by what he had told her.

'She recovered for a short while but she was in a wheelchair.' Garth stared at her. 'She needed me, Sabrina, and I felt so goddamned guilty.'

'So you finished with my mother?'

He nodded. 'It was the hardest thing I've ever had to do.' There was a far-away look in his eyes for a moment. 'She must have known that she was pregnant when I finished with her, but she never told me.'

'I suppose she didn't want you to feel trapped.'

'Yes, I suppose so.' He smiled sadly. 'The awful thing was that Jessica died six months later. But by that time your mother had moved and I had no idea where she was.'

Sabrina lowered her eyes from his and there was silence for a moment as both were lost in their own private worlds.

Then she looked up at him sadly. 'I sometimes think that fate chooses the paths for our lives. Maybe you and my mother were just never meant to be.'

'Maybe. About four years later I met Nadine. She was a widow with a young son and I was a widower.' He smiled at Sabrina. 'We comforted each other and I fell very much in love with her. I never did tell her about my affair with your mother. She was so sympathetic about my losing my wife—how could I tell her that I had been unfaithful to her?' Garth shook his head. 'Even now I feel guilty when I think about Jessica.'

Sabrina understood Garth's reluctance to tell Nadine. Maybe if he had told her right at the beginning that his marriage to Jessica had been a mistake she would have understood. But to have to tell her now would be hard.

'Anyway I thought that I would never see your mother again and then one day I bumped into her in the middle of Oxford Street. I could hardly believe my eyes. It was six years since I had last seen her. We went and had a drink together.' Garth pushed a shaking hand through his hair. 'I told her I was married with a baby daughter and a stepson. She told me about you. You can imagine my shock.'

Sabrina could indeed.

'I don't know, Sabrina, maybe I let you down and maybe I took the coward's way out, but when she told me that things were better left as they were I agreed with her.'

Sabrina blinked back sudden tears.

'She had already told you that your father was dead. And I had to consider Nadine. I do love her——'

'It's all right, Garth. I understand,' she broke across him hastily, understanding him and loving him for being so upset, for caring about what she thought.

He smiled at her. 'When I needed a secretary and I knew you were looking for a job I couldn't resist asking your mother to point you in my direction. I wanted so much to know you. I wasn't disappointed by the young woman I met.'

His eyes moved gently over her face, noting the emotion in the deep blue eyes, and he placed a comforting arm around her shoulder. 'I'm sorry I've made a mess of things,' he whispered softly. 'That I've upset you so much.'

'It's a relief to know everything, to be honest.' She smiled tremulously at him.

He smiled back. 'It's your birthday on Saturday, isn't it?' he asked suddenly.

She nodded, surprised that he knew. She had almost forgotten about it herself, there had been so much on her mind recently.

'Let me take you out somewhere to celebrate. Lunch or dinner; you choose.'

Sabrina hesitated for a moment and bit down sharply on her lip; she felt totally out of her depth with all of this. 'I don't know, Garth...'

'You don't want me in your life, is that it?' His voice sounded unbearably strained.

'I...no.' She shook her head. 'No, it's not that at all.' If the truth were known, Sabrina desperately wanted Garth in her life. She wanted to know her father. She stumbled, then looked up at him with wide glimmering eyes. 'But let's face it, Garth, the situation is a mess. Your family don't know about your affair with my mother or about me. You are a man who is very much in the public eye. Can you really afford to have me in your life?'

He was silent for a moment. 'I admit that I'm scared about telling Nadine and, yes, my career is important and it is in a difficult period of transition at the moment.'

She nodded. 'I understand more than you think, Garth. Even a whisper of scandal could be very damaging to you at the moment.'

He knew that what she was saying was right—she could see it in the over-bright gleam of his eyes. 'You could still come to Brussels with me as my secretary. Then when things have settled down...'

She shook her head.

'Think about it, Brina.' He reached across and took hold of her hand. 'Please.'

Her eyes shone with tears. 'Oh, Garth, I just don't know anything any more.'

'Come on,' he said gently. 'Let's walk some more.' He tucked his arm around her shoulder as she shivered suddenly.

Both of them were so caught up in their conversation that they didn't see the man who was leaning against a tree at the bottom of the garden, a zoom-lens camera trained directly on them.

CHAPTER THREE

SABRINA had never been as nervous about a date as she was about lunch with Marc Kingsley. She paid special attention to her hair and make-up that day and took ages deciding what to wear.

She decided finally on a cream linen suit that had a short skirt and a long-line jacket. She teamed it with a peach silk blouse. The effect was both stylish and yet sensual. As she surveyed her appearance in the mirror she was comforted by the fact that she looked serene and calm. She would hate Marc to know just what chaos he had wrought to her system by that one kiss.

The effects of that kiss still remained with her now. She could feel heat rising inside her when she remembered how she had pressed close against him, how soft and skilled his mouth had felt against hers. She swallowed hard as she tried to dismiss the memory.

When the front doorbell rang she felt her stomach tying itself into knots. With a last glance in the mirror she went to let him in.

'Good morning.' Marc's manner was brisk, but the eyes that swept over her appearance were very complimentary.

'Would you like a coffee or anything before we leave?' Sabrina invited softly.

He shook his head. 'No time.'

'Oh?'

He ignored the question in her eyes and smiled. 'Are you ready?'

She nodded and turned to pick up her handbag.

'And don't forget your passport,' he said casually.

'My passport...' She looked around at him in complete surprise. 'Why do I need that?'

'If you run along and get it, I'll tell you on the way,' he said with infuriating calm.

Sabrina's hand wasn't quite steady as she opened the drawer of her bureau and took out her passport. Where on earth was he taking her? she wondered. Her heart thudded with a mixture of excitement and apprehension. Even a lunch date with Marc Kingsley felt like an adventure.

He looked exceptionally stylish this morning. He was wearing a dark suit that seemed to emphasise his dark good looks, his hair gleaming almost blue-black in the spring sunshine.

She was surprised to find that he wasn't in his red Porsche this morning. Instead a long black limousine waited at the kerb, and a uniformed chauffeur held the door for them as they climbed into the luxurious seats.

'This is very decadent.' Sabrina smiled at Marc a little shyly.

'Practical,' he told her crisply. 'I find it easier to have a chauffeur when I make business trips. I can carry on with my work as we travel and I don't waste any time.'

'I see.' Her eyebrows rose slightly. 'Am I to take it we are on a business trip?'

He pursed his lips thoughtfully. 'No, I just don't want to waste time.' Then he grinned at her. It was a deliciously wicked grin that did incredible things to her heart-rate.

'Champagne?' He leaned forward and pulled down a cabinet in front of them. Packed very neatly inside there were rows of bottles and crystal glasses, including a silver bucket with a chilled bottle of champagne.

'It's a little early for me,' Sabrina murmured. She wasn't used to drinking in the middle of the day at the best of times and, accompanied by such a suave, handsome man, she was frightened of lowering any of her barriers...especially to Marc Kingsley.

'Nonsense.' The champagne cork flew off with an almighty pop and the champagne flowed with frothy enthusiasm into two crystal glasses. 'It's never too early to start celebrating.' He handed her the glass and she accepted it with only a moment's pause.

'What are we celebrating?' she asked, wrinkling her nose as bubbles tickled it.

For a moment he considered her question. 'Why, spring of course and the rising sap.'

She caught his eye and had to laugh. 'You are incorrigible, Marc Kingsley,' she said with a shake of her head.

'I hope so.' He reached across to top up her glass as she took a drink from its golden contents.

'I hope you're not trying to get me drunk,' she said in a mock-teasing voice, 'because it won't work.'

One dark eyebrow rose at that. 'My dear girl, I have never had to stoop so low.' This time there was no laughter in his tone.

Sabrina could well believe it, and immediately she felt a little embarrassed at making such a comment.

'Anyway, what do you mean, it won't work?' he went on to ask, the laughter back in his eyes.

Sabrina smiled and let the question pass without comment. 'So where are we going for lunch?'

'A lovely little restaurant I know on the Left Bank.'

For a moment Sabrina was puzzled. 'The left bank of what?'

'The Seine,' he said matter-of-factly.

'The Seine...in Paris?' Her voice rose a little with the thrill of it.

'No, in Clacton,' he said with a teasing light in his eyes. 'Yes, of course, Paris,' he finished with a grin. 'Where else would we go on such a magnificent spring day?'

She smiled and matched his nonchalant tone. 'Of course...where else?'

Sabrina had never experienced such a day before. Marc was so amusing and so laid-back about everything. He whisked her into the first-class lounge at the airport and then almost immediately they were on board the aircraft. From then it was just half an hour before they were putting down in Paris.

She was on her third glass of champagne by the time they were being chauffeur-driven along the banks of the River Seine.

'I can't believe this,' Sabrina murmured as she looked out at the sparkling water and the majestic buildings lit with the brilliance of spring sunshine.

'Can't you?' He looked across at her, and then to her surprise he reached for her hand and pressed it close to his lips. 'I could offer you the world, Sabrina,' he said huskily. 'Whatever you want, I could give you.'

Her heart seemed to flutter in some strange way as she looked into his eyes. She didn't want anything, she realised with one strange jolt. It was enough to have him look at her like that.

She pulled her hand away from his, confused by her emotions. She couldn't afford to get involved with Marc Kingsley, she told herself fiercely. This was a one-off. For the sake of her father, she had to remember that.

'Have I said something wrong?' he asked softly.

'No...' She shook her head, then forced herself to smile at him.

He didn't return her smile. 'I take it you are thinking about the other man in your life?' His deep voice was suddenly spiced with an emotion Sabrina found hard to define.

'No...' She shook her head, but she could tell he wasn't convinced. His lean features had a hard look to them suddenly, and his eyes glittered with cold, harsh light.

'You're a fool, Sabrina... he won't leave his wife for you,' he said grimly.

For a moment she was so stunned that she couldn't answer him. 'What... what on earth makes you think I would go out with a married man?' she spluttered at last.

He shrugged nonchalantly. 'It was just a passing notion.'

'Well, I would let it pass if I were you,' she said in a very angry tone.

He looked at her closely. It was so hard to tell what went on behind those cool, watchful eyes, she thought with a shiver.

'If that's what you want,' he said at last.

'Yes, it is.' Sabrina frowned indignantly. Why had he assumed she was seeing a married man?

'Come on.' Marc leaned forward and tapped the glass partition. 'You can leave us here,' he said to the driver. 'Pick us up at the restaurant at about four.'

The car pulled smoothly to a halt. 'We may as well walk from here,' Marc said, holding out a hand to her as she moved towards the door.

She ignored his outstretched hand and alighted to the pavement without help.

'You're not going to spend the rest of the afternoon in a sulk, are you, Sabrina?' he asked as he closed the door and the limousine pulled away from them into the busy flow of traffic.

She caught his eye and then smiled. 'I don't sulk. I was just irritated that you could make such a rash assumption.'

'I've made my fortune by them,' he said in a dry voice. 'You will have to forgive me.'

'I'll think about it.' But she was already forgetting about it. It was such a glorious day. The sun sparkled over the wide boulevards with their grand buildings, the horse chestnuts were starting to unfurl their green banners; the feeling of spring was everywhere.

'I love this time of year,' she said, breathing in deeply.

His lips tugged into a lazy smile and he reached for her hand. 'It's a time for lovers to stroll hand in hand,' he said in a low tone that sent Sabrina's heart into overdrive.

She didn't try to pull away from him; instead she allowed herself to savour the feeling of his warm skin next to hers. They walked along the banks of the Seine in silence for a while and for a moment Sabrina felt more relaxed than she had for a long time.

'How old are you, Marc?' she asked suddenly.

He looked at her with an amused glint in his eyes. 'Thirty-six ... why?'

She shrugged. 'I was just wondering about you, that's all.'

'What were you wondering?'

'Well . . . why you're not married . . . don't you want to settle down, have children?' It must have been the champagne. She would never have asked him such a question ordinarily.

To her surprise he considered her question. 'I would like children one day,' he said seriously. 'I've just never met anyone I want to settle down with.'

'Garth says you are a heartbreaker.' The words just slipped out and she regretted them immediately.

'Does he now?' Marc's voice was arid.

'Oh, don't get me wrong. Garth thinks the world of you,' she continued hurriedly. 'He was just…concerned.'

'That you might fall for me?' He looked at her with a strange expression in his eyes.

'No…' Sabrina trailed off, wishing she had never started this conversation.

'Did you tell Garth you were coming out with me today?' he asked abruptly.

'Yes, of course.' Sabrina looked over at Marc. For a moment his expression looked harsh and remote, then he caught her watching him and smiled, making her wonder if she had imagined that look.

'Are you hungry?' he asked now.

She nodded. It was amazing but she was; for the first time in ages she had a real appetite.

They ate lunch in a beautiful restaurant that looked out over the river. It had a stylish ambience and Sabrina was very glad that she had taken so much trouble over her appearance that day.

The food was excellent. Sabrina chose seafood while Marc went for steak washed down with some excellent wine.

Later, as she listened to him speaking French to the waiters, Sabrina was reminded forcibly that he was half French and that he lived most of the time out here. He wasn't in London very often. That thought upset her more than she had thought possible. How ridiculous, she chided herself. She couldn't get involved with Marc anyway. It wasn't fair to Garth and it wasn't fair to Marc. You couldn't possibly have any kind of relationship with a man that you had to keep such a large secret from.

He looked across and caught her watching him. 'What are you thinking?' he asked, his eyes moving over her delicate face and locking on the huge sparkling blue of her eyes.

'I was just remembering that this is home territory for you,' she said with a shrug, trying very hard to keep her rather foolish thoughts to herself.

'Yes, it is. My mother is originally from Paris. My father was English, though ... from Cheshire. But they made their home out here.'

The waiter brought them coffee and cognac. 'I'll show you around my house later,' Marc said as they were left alone again. She nodded. She was filled with an avid curiosity to know more about Marc Kingsley. He fascinated her as no other man had ever done.

'Do you have offices in London, Marc?' she asked curiously, wondering how often he got over to England.

'Yes ... but my main offices are here in Paris.' He finished his coffee and motioned to the waiter for the bill. 'That's why I would like you to come out here and work for me,' he added casually.

Sabrina's eyes flew to his face. Was he joking?

'I believe you speak five languages fluently,' he said with a lift of one dark eyebrow. 'Someone who could speak German, French, Dutch would be invaluable to me.'

Sabrina's smile faded a little. Was this why he had brought her out for lunch? Was he more interested in her work abilities than he was in her? She was surprised by how much that idea hurt...but it was ridiculous to be upset. After all there was nothing between them; there would never be anything between them.

'Yes...I can, but——'

He cut across her abruptly. 'Don't say anything yet, Sabrina, not until you have heard my offer and given it some consideration.'

She nodded. 'All right, Marc.' But deep down inside she knew she wasn't at liberty even to consider his offer. Garth would find the prospect of her working with his stepson too much of a strain, and if she was honest she knew she would too.

The limousine was waiting outside for them and they made themselves comfortable in the leather seats as they drove once more through the busy traffic. For a little while neither of them spoke. Sabrina was too engrossed in her own thoughts to notice the way Marc was watching her, a deeply contemplative expression in his dark eyes.

It wasn't long before Paris was left behind and lush countryside opened up before them. Then the limousine turned through an imposing gateway and down a long drive lined with poplar trees.

'My home,' Marc said as she gasped with pleasure at the building in front of them.

Marc's home was like something out of a fairy-tale. It was a very large château with rounded towers at either end. Behind it was the dark green of a forest, in front the most beautiful gardens and fountains.

The limousine glided to a halt in front of the enormous studded front door and Marc got out first, then turned to take her hand.

He didn't release her hand but kept hold of her as they walked up and into the house.

The splendour of the hallway was such that it was overwhelming. The magnificent staircase that curved gently into the centre of the hallway was ornately carved in gold and carpeted in a rich red.

'Your home is breathtaking,' Sabrina said in a low tone as she looked around.

He nodded. 'I fell in love with it immediately. Apparently it is an almost perfect example of the Renaissance period. Come on, I'll show you around.'

Each room was more beautiful than the one before. It was furnished with priceless antiques and the paintings alone must have been worth a fortune.

Sabrina stopped to admire a particularly lovely painting on the landing at the top of the stairs.

'That is one of my favourites,' Marc said casually from beside her. 'It's a Pre-Raphaelite actually.'

'Was the château already furnished when you bought it?' Sabrina asked curiously as they continued down a long corridor.

'Yes...I've added to it as I've gone along, with the paintings mostly.' He opened a door at the far end of the corridor. 'Now I think this room will interest you.'

The bedroom that he led her into was superb. It was built in the tower section of the house and had a round window-seat at the far end that looked out over a spectacular view. A four-poster bed dominated the room. Its canopy was a heavy gold and blue tapestry, colours that were echoed in the carpet and curtains.

'They say that Napoleon and Josephine stayed here for a weekend of passion.' Marc crossed and sat on the edge of the bed. 'What do you think?' He looked up at her with that hard, searching look that made her heart go into overdrive.

She could feel her face growing hot as his eyes moved over her. 'I think it's very beautiful,' she managed to say primly, and walked over to look out of the windows at the view, trying desperately to gather her senses.

She was aware of Marc moving to stand behind her. 'Do you like my home, Sabrina?' he asked softly.

'You know I do.' She twisted her hands nervously.

His hand touched her shoulder. 'I'm glad...I've enjoyed your company very much today.'

'Oh, Marc!' For a moment, to her dismay, she felt like crying. 'Today has been wonderful. I wish...' She trailed off, at a loss. Her voice was low and filled with confusion.

'What do you wish, Sabrina?' His voice sounded so gentle and deep.

She took a deep breath and pulled herself together sharply. She wished that things could be different. That Garth could openly be the father she so desperately needed. That there could be a chance for her to develop a relationship with Marc. She shook her head sadly, knowing that wasn't possible. 'That it didn't have to end,' she whispered in a trembling tone.

'It doesn't have to.' His voice was a husky murmur as his hand moved to stroke her strawberry-blonde hair in a tantalising, seductive way.

'Yes, it does.' She turned to look at him with wide, glimmering eyes. 'Today has been one of the happiest days I can remember for a long time,' she whispered softly. 'I want to thank you for that, Marc.'

His eyes raked over her pale complexion, at the tears that shimmered in her beautiful eyes. 'Poor darling,' he said softly, lifting a hand to smooth away a tear as it glistened on her cheek. 'You've gone through a difficult time recently, haven't you?'

The sympathy in his tone was almost her undoing…she could have broken down there and then and told him everything.

'I know what you are going through,' he continued softly. 'I felt wretched and very mixed up after my father died.' His hand moved to her waist and he pulled her close against the hard line of his body, holding her and stroking her back.

It was wonderful just to be held like that. She leaned her head against his chest; she could hear the steady beat of his heart—hers was racing in a much wilder fashion.

'Come out to Paris and start a new life, Sabrina,' he whispered against her ear.

She pulled away from him and looked up at him in confusion.

'You can have a new job…an apartment here.' He stroked her hair back from her face. 'We can get to know each other.'

She closed her eyes, allowing herself to savour the idea for a moment before she shook her head. 'I…I can't, Marc.'

'I can give you more than you've ever dreamed of, Sabrina.' When his head bent and his lips touched hers, she felt as if everything inside her was melting with pleasure.

It was just a gentle kiss; she was the one to deepen it. She reached up and curled her fingers through his hair and gave herself up to the heady pleasure of his caress. Her mouth felt hungry against his...she wanted so much more. It was incredible how easily he could arouse her. Her body ached with a kind of white-hot sensuality she hadn't known she possessed.

There was just a moment's hesitation on his part. Then he returned her kisses with a fierceness that swept her even further away from the edge of sanity.

When he pulled away from her she could see surprise in his dark eyes. She felt her soft lips curve in a trembling smile. She felt surprised herself...there was a chemistry between them that defied logic. She hardly knew this man yet her whole body ached for him in a way that she had never known.

'Will you think over my offer?' he asked in a low tone.

She hesitated. Everything inside her screamed yes, but rational thought threw in a note of caution and reality. 'I...oh, Marc.' For just a moment there was a note of despair in her voice.

He stared down at her. The light was fading outside now and she couldn't see his features clearly. 'Just forget the other man in your life, Sabrina.' There was a grim note to his voice now.

'If only it were that simple,' she said sadly, thinking of Garth, of how much he had to lose if the truth about her ever slipped out.

'It is that simple.' He reached out and caught hold of her arm. His grip was strong and it bit into her flesh. 'Believe me, I know.'

'Marc...you're hurting me.' She frowned at the expression in his voice, the grip on her arm.

'Am I?' His voice softened and he released her. Yet for one moment Sabrina had the curious feeling that he had meant to hurt her. She didn't like the idea; it sent a chill wave of fear racing through her.

He trailed one finger softly down her cheek. 'Life could be so sweet, Sabrina,' he whispered in a husky tone.

Immediately the foolish notion of fear melted.

'There is the most beautiful apartment waiting for you. Next week you could be driving around Paris in a new sports car. You could have expense accounts at the best fashion houses. You and I could deepen our relationship...' He let his voice drift away meaningfully.

For a moment she just stared up at him. Sabrina didn't care for the mercenary ring to those words. She wasn't the type of person to be lured by material goods. It was his strength...his compassion...yes, his passion that she craved at that moment.

'I don't need those things, Marc,' she whispered. 'I——'

'Yes, you do, Sabrina,' he cut across her forcibly. 'Life could be very easy or life could be difficult...it's your choice.'

Sabrina frowned. She didn't understand what he was saying or that note in his voice.

It was practically dark in the room, so it was hard to tell what Marc was thinking. His face was shadowed.

He looked stern and not at all like the charming, gentle man who had warmed her heart today.

'Marc...' Her voice was almost pleading. 'I don't know what you mean. I——'

The shrill ring of a phone cut across her.

He sighed and moved away from her to pick it up. 'Yes?' His voice was abrupt and not at all pleasant. 'I see.' He reached out a hand and warm golden light spilled from the table-lamp over his face and his dark hair.

'All right...it can't be helped.' He raked a hand through his hair.

He looked tired, Sabrina thought suddenly. He glanced across at her and their eyes met and held.

'All right...I'll be out there in the morning.' Marc put the receiver down.

'I'm sorry, Sabrina,' he murmured, 'but I won't be able to accompany you back to London. I'm going to have to go to Germany first thing tomorrow. I have problems with a new factory I'm buying.'

Disappointment flooded her.

He walked across and touched her cheek. 'I'm sorry, darling.'

Immediately she felt like curling up in his arms, resting her head against his broad chest. The confusion and fear that had circled her heart a moment ago were forgotten. She had been imagining things...it had been the half-light playing silly tricks on her imagination. Now, in the soft gold light, Marc looked incredibly gentle and wonderful again.

'I'll take you to the airport and my chauffeur will meet you and take you home,' he continued softly. 'Is that all right?'

'Yes...yes, of course.' She wanted to ask when she would see him again, but that was a leading question into a relationship that couldn't lead anywhere.

CHAPTER FOUR

FOR the next few days Sabrina was haunted by thoughts of Marc Kingsley. One moment she was thinking about the way he kissed her, the next about his offer to go and live in Paris.

Her emotions swam around and around in a muddle of confusion. One moment she was melting inside and ready to fly to Paris at the first signal from Marc. The next moment she was in black despair.

She was particularly depressed after a phone call from Garth. The first thing he had asked her about was her lunch with Marc. His voice had sounded so anxious that it had just torn at Sabrina's heart.

'You didn't let anything slip, did you, Brina?' he had said softly. 'I mean about us, about——'

'No, Garth, please don't worry. I would never say anything,' she had been quick to reassure him.

'Are you going to see him again?'

The question had torn at Sabrina's ragged nerves. She wanted to tell him no... but her heart refused to let her say the word. 'I... I don't know,' she'd said at last.

He had sighed. 'I'm sorry, Sabrina... this is all my fault. I've put you in an impossible situation.'

'No... please don't worry, Garth. It's not important.'

Liar, a little inner voice had whispered.

Garth, however, had sounded a little happier after she had told him that. 'Have you thought any more about coming back to work for me?' he had asked gently.

'I've thought about it...I don't know, Garth,' she'd said nervously.

'We'll talk about it when I take you out on your birthday,' he had said firmly. 'I'll pick you up at about midday on Saturday.'

Sabrina had spent hours deliberating what to do after that. Should she go back to work for Garth? There was a big part of her that wanted to very much. She wanted to get to know her father...she wanted him in her life.

Then Marc Kingsley's dark face rose in her thoughts. She remembered walking hand in hand along the banks of the River Seine with him. She remembered how he had held her and the sensations that had raced through her body. Then she remembered the drive to the airport.

Marc had been very quiet on that journey, his face impassive, his dark eyes staring straight ahead as the limousine cut through the darkness of the night towards Paris.

He had walked with her to the terminal and she had stood slightly apart from him. Her heart had thudded painfully as she had said goodbye to him.

'Remember what I said, Sabrina,' he had said quietly. 'Life could be very sweet.'

Those words had played and replayed through her mind on that journey home, along with the fact that he hadn't kissed her goodbye...just touched her face, the strangest expression on his face.

That was four days ago and she hadn't heard from him since. With a sigh Sabrina tried to put him out of her mind. What was the use of torturing herself with thoughts of him? She couldn't get involved.

She busied herself for the rest of that day sorting through some boxes that she had brought from her mother's house. Lucy Harrington had lived in a large house in Richmond and Sabrina had been left with the rather daunting task of clearing it out ready to sell it.

Under the terms of her mother's will the house was to be sold and part of the proceeds was to go to cancer research, a cause that had always been close to Lucy Harrington since she had lost her sister to the disease. The remainder of the money was left to Sabrina. It meant that she would have no money worries for the fore-seeable future.

Given a choice Sabrina would have preferred not to sell the property... not for a while at least. She found it very painful to have to go through her mother's pos-sessions. The task of getting rid of her mother's clothes and personal items was the hardest job she had ever had to undertake.

Even now, going through several tea chests of books and ornaments, she felt like crying. It had been an afternoon like this when she had found her mother's diary. She would never forget the shock, the incredulity, of reading that book. Just thinking about it now made her hands shake.

The ring of the telephone was a welcome relief and she reached for it blindly. 'Hello?' Her voice sounded husky and emotional even to her own ears.

'Sabrina... everything all right?' It was Marc's brisk tone.

A warm feeling flowed through her immediately. 'Marc, this is a nice surprise.' Her voice sounded bright and cheerful now.

'Expecting someone else to call, were you?' he asked somewhat drily.

She frowned. 'No... what do you mean?'

'Nothing.' For a moment there was a silence.

'Thank you once again for a lovely day out,' she said awkwardly to cover the lull in the conversation.

'Have you thought over my offer?'

The crisply authoritative voice startled her. It was hardly the voice to use when trying to woo someone.

'Well——' she paused '—I don't think it's the right time for me to think about moving to Paris, Marc.' Her eyes moved over the boxes in front of her. She had to be sensible. She had a lot still to sort out here in London, and Garth would be incredibly upset and worried if she said she was leaving to spend time with his stepson. In her mind she knew it would be wrong to move; in her heart... her heart was sore just with the effort of trying to be practical.

He didn't answer her immediately, and when he did his voice was harsh. 'Think very carefully before turning me down, Sabrina.'

'Don't you think I have?' For a moment there was a note of anguish in her tone.

Silence greeted her statement. 'I'll speak to you later,' he grated and then abruptly the line went dead.

Sabrina stared at the phone, puzzled by Marc's mood. He had sounded so distant... almost threatening.

She shook her head and went back to her work. Maybe he was just upset, the thought cheered her a little. If he was upset then he cared about her.

She raked a trembling hand through her hair and went back to her task. It was best to keep busy... not to think too deeply about anything.

A few hours later she found an old photograph album full of pictures of her mother and herself when she had been just a toddler, and her emotions spilled over. If only she had her mother to talk to about Marc, about her father. She felt so confused, so mixed up about everything.

With a heavy heart Sabrina cleared away the boxes and went to have a relaxing bath. The warm, soapy water made her feel a little better and, wrapping herself in a towelling robe, she went downstairs to make herself a snack before turning in for the night.

She was just in the process of heating some milk in the hope that it would make her sleep when the doorbell rang.

Frowning, she went out to the hallway and glanced at the clock nervously. It was nearly ten-thirty... who on earth would be ringing her bell at this hour?

Apprehensively she went to the door and, putting the safety-chain on, opened it a crack.

'Sabrina, it's Marc.' The familiar brisk tone sent a wave of panic through her. She didn't want to see Marc Kingsley, not when she was dressed like this.

'For heaven's sake open the door,' he commanded in a rather imperious voice.

Against her better judgement, she opened the door fully. 'Marc, what are you doing here at this hour?' She tried very hard to sound cool and collected as her eyes moved over his broad-shouldered frame. He was dressed in a heavy overcoat, the collar turned up against the chill night air. He looked cold and a little tired.

'If you let me in, I'll tell you,' he grated, a trifle impatiently.

With mixed feelings, she stood back and allowed him in. Part of her was ecstatic to see him, part of her was strangely frightened.

He took off his coat and threw it casually over the banisters. He looked incredibly handsome, his dark hair ruffled from the night wind, a few raindrops glistening on his tanned skin.

'Are you going to ask me into your lounge or are you expecting your boyfriend?' His dark eyes raked over her scathingly, taking in everything from the soft blue dressing-gown to the unruly state of her strawberry-blonde hair.

She literally flinched at that look in his eyes and her nerves suddenly felt as if they were at screaming point.

'Why, Marc, you sound jealous!' Somehow she managed to match his rather sardonic tone.

He made a vaguely contemptuous sound which didn't help to dull the anger that was starting to rise inside her. She didn't like the way he was talking to her...what had she done to put that look in his eyes? Her heart slammed painfully against her chest.

Then he raked a hand through his thick dark hair and shrugged. 'Well, aren't you going to offer me a drink? I could murder a whisky.'

She hesitated and then with a sigh turned to lead the way into the lounge. She had to admit that she was very curious to find out why he was paying her a call at this hour of the night, why his mood seemed so black.

The room was warm and cosy, a fire burning in the Adam-style fireplace, a soothing classical tape playing on the stereo.

He stood by the fireplace and watched her pour his drink with eyes that didn't miss the slight tremble of her hands.

'So... am I to take it from our conversation today that you have no intention of taking me up on my offer of a job?' he asked briskly.

Was that all it had been—just an offer of a job? She had thought... had hoped that it had been something more than that. 'Is that why you are here?' She crossed the room to hand him his drink, meeting his eyes with great difficulty.

'Yes, of course.' He took a sip of his drink and put it down on the coffee-table next to the settee.

She bit down on her lip. Lord, but Marc Kingsley was a cool customer. 'Well, I'm sorry, Marc, but I have to turn down your proposition.' She kept the hurt and confusion out of her tone with extreme difficulty and tilted her head proudly. She didn't deserve to be treated like this. If he had just wanted to employ her he should have said so... he should not have led her on or kissed her the way he had. Lord, the thought of that kiss made her temperature rise.

'That's a great pity.' He spoke very quietly, yet there was an immense feeling of menace to his tone. 'I was hoping that with gentle persuasion I might get you to stay on in Paris. But you are obviously a shrewd lady, one who isn't going to be lured away so easily.'

She frowned. 'Look, Marc, I've told you that I can't work for you. That should be enough. I haven't time for games.' Suddenly she was losing her patience. He had no right coming around here trying to make her feel guilty for not accepting his job. And what did he mean, he had tried to lure her away? Away from what, for heaven's sake?

'I would have thought that a woman like you would always have time for games,' he drawled laconically.

'A woman like me?' She stared at him, completely nonplussed now. 'What on earth do you mean by that?'

He moved a step nearer to her and she had the strangest sensation of being backed into a corner. She took a step back from him as he stopped in front of her.

'You know what I mean,' he said slowly and deliberately. 'I'm referring to your relationship with Garth.'

Shock flowed through her. She didn't know what she had expected him to say, but it certainly wasn't this! For a moment she could only stare at him. Wild colour lit her cheeks and her heart thudded loudly and painfully in her chest. How had he found out? Had Garth told him?

'You see, you do know what I mean.' He reached out a hand to trail a finger softly down the side of her face. She flinched from the contact and her skin seemed to burn from his touch. 'I wish I could say that I can't see what the attraction is,' Marc continued, his voice deep and steady, 'but I can see it all too clearly.' His fingers moved under her chin, tipping her face up towards the brutal scrutiny of his eyes.

'What...what on earth are you talking about?' She put up a hand to try and ward him away from her but he merely moved and caught it in a vice-like grip that made her gasp with pain.

'I'm talking about the fact that my stepfather is having an affair with you,' he answered calmly.

'What?' She stopped struggling to free her hand and stared up at him. 'How dare you...how dare you say something so disgusting, so absurd?' Her voice was low and trembling with rage. She just couldn't believe what he had just said. Then suddenly everything fell into place.

This was why he had offered to set her up in his apartment in Paris! She raked a hand through her hair. Heavens, how blind she had been. She had thought it was because he was attracted to her...that he wanted to get to know her. She found herself remembering how passionately she had responded to his kisses, and her lips twisted in self-mockery at how naïvely stupid she had been. Never for one moment had she guessed that he suspected something so vile...that he had been deliberately trying to lure her away from Garth.

His gaze raked over the white pallor of her skin, her large eyes that seemed to have changed from blue to deepest violet. 'I applaud your acting, Sabrina,' he murmured. 'Disgusting?' He pursed his lips as if thinking over her words. 'Maybe, maybe not, but absurd it certainly is not.'

He released her hand and his eyes moved down over the slender lines of her figure in the blue towelling robe, making her whole body stiffen with outrage. 'As I said, I can understand the attraction. You are a very desirable young woman. I can even understand why you would choose Garth. He is kind, gentle, also very rich. I am sure that the rewards from such an association are far greater than the...shall we say?...efforts you must put in.'

Her hand swung back and she would have caught him a stinging blow across the face were it not for the fact that his reflexes were sharper than hers, and he captured her slender arm in one strong hand before it got anywhere near him.

'That is not advisable, my dear,' he drawled calmly. 'Childish tantrums are going to get you nowhere.'

For a moment she was so incensed with him that she felt like kicking out at him. The dark gaze narrowed almost as if he could read her mind and she found herself pulling away from him and taking a step back.

'Good.' The well-shaped lips twisted in an arrogant smile. 'I'm glad that you are going to be sensible. You'll find that I am a reasonable man.'

She decided not to give him the satisfaction of a reply and stood glaring at him with mutinous contempt.

'Perhaps the fact that I am half French makes it easier for me to understand this affair,' he continued smoothly. 'Some of the French think of it as an acceptable fact for a man to keep a mistress, but I don't think my mother would fall into that category. It took her a long time to get over my father's death and Garth has been like a lifeline to her out of that sadness. She loves him very much and I believe that Garth feels the same way about her.'

'Nadine doesn't think... you haven't told her——?' Sabrina was so horrified that she could barely get her words out.

'No.' He cut in across her breathless questions. 'She doesn't know that her husband is having an affair, but she does know that something is wrong. She confided as much to me only a couple of months ago.'

'And you have put two and two together and have come up with six,' Sabrina muttered acidly.

'Do not insult my intelligence, Sabrina.' His voice was low but his eyes glittered with fury, the hard line of his jaw was tense and she knew, for all his calm, controlled words, that underneath his anger was simmering. 'Once I realised that Garth's problems were not work-related or financial it didn't take me long to discover there was another woman on the scene, especially when I found out that Garth had purchased another apartment. An apartment that his wife knows nothing about.'

Sabrina frowned, genuinely puzzled at this. 'What apartment? What are you talking about?'

'Don't bat those wide, innocent eyes at me, darling,' he drawled heavily, 'because I know you exactly for what you are. This beautiful apartment that we stand in was bought by Garth Fraiser over five years ago for an astronomical amount of money. He sold it to you for a fraction of the money.'

Sabrina stared at him, her mouth literally open. She had thought that this apartment in Kensington had been a good buy, a bargain. She had never for one moment suspected that there was anything untoward about it.

'You've been having an affair with Garth for five years and last year he installed you at his office as his secretary——'

'No,' she interrupted him vehemently. 'Marc, you have got to believe me, I am not having an affair with your stepfather, and you have got it all wrong about my apartment, and everything.'

'How much did you pay for this place?' he enquired abruptly.

Even as she told him the sum she knew that it was ludicrously low, even for so many years ago. She had questioned it at the time and her mother had told her just to buy it quickly before the person who owned it changed his mind.

Marc's harsh laughter grated on her over-stretched nerves.

'I've always thought that Garth had a good sense of humour.'

She watched his dark, arrogant face with silent fury. 'You've got it all wrong,' she muttered after a while.

'Oh, I don't think so. I have been investigating you for weeks now.' He smiled down at her very coolly. 'And I saw you in Garth's arms only the other day out in his garden.'

He reached into his inside pocket and took out some photographs to hand to her. She took them in numb fingers . . . she could hardly believe this. Looking down, she saw close-up shots taken of her and Garth out in his garden. One of him putting a comforting arm around her . . . although in the photograph it looked like an amorous embrace. One of him wiping a tear away from her cheek.

'You seem to make a habit of crying on men's shoulders, don't you, Sabrina?' he grated drily.

She blanched at that cruel blatant reminder of how she had cried in front of him at his house in Paris.

'I was upset,' she said huskily.

'A ploy that works very well,' he grated roughly. 'You almost had me feeling sorry for you.'

She blanched at the callous remark. She had been so taken in by his deep voice filled with sympathy, and all along he had despised her . . . had felt nothing but contempt. She felt utterly foolish and incredibly hurt.

'I can't believe that you would stoop so low as to take these pictures!' she whispered in a low, trembling voice.

'I hired a private detective to do some digging,' he said coolly. 'He took those.'

'You disgust me.' She glared at him with eyes that spoke volumes, and then in sheer fury she threw the photographs at him. 'These prove nothing.'

'I disagree. Do you know what a photograph like that could do to my stepfather's reputation? To his career?' His voice was contemptuous.

She had a pretty good idea and she shuddered at the thought. 'I think maybe you had better leave,' she said now in a tightly controlled voice. It was obvious that she was not going to be able to change Marc's opinion of her until she told him the truth, and that was something she couldn't do until she had spoken to Garth.

'You must be joking. I'm not going anywhere until we have this sorted out.' There was a menacing undercurrent in his voice that made her suddenly very nervous.

'There is nothing to sort out.' She couldn't quite hide the tremble in her voice, and to make up for it she lifted her head defiantly. 'So what if I bought my apartment from Garth? It means nothing, and as for those photos they are just of two friends enjoying a walk. Nothing more.'

The false bravado died a quick death as he took a step nearer. 'I'm warning you, Sabrina, my patience has limits.'

Her cheeks flared with colour. He really frightened her when he spoke like that. She stared up at him with wide, scared eyes. 'It's not what you're thinking, Marc,' she said in a strained voice.

He raked an impatient hand through his hair. 'Those baby blues of yours don't work on me,' he grated sardonically. He grabbed hold of her arm and moved her forcefully towards a chair. 'Let's just get down to business, shall we? My time is too valuable to waste on someone of your calibre.'

It took all her self-control not to hurl the truth at him at that moment, that plus a few insulting remarks of her own. To think that she had actually felt attracted to this man once! He had to be the most insufferable brute she had ever met. Absently she rubbed at her arm, which was throbbing from the rough way he had held it, and glared at him. If looks could kill he should be flat on his back by now, she thought with a small measure of satisfaction.

'Sit down,' he commanded abruptly.

She didn't need to be told twice—no one in their right mind would have argued with that tone of voice.

'So... how much will you accept?'

'I beg your pardon?' She had to tip her head back now to look up at him.

He raked an impatient hand through thick dark hair. 'We have established the fact that you are a scheming hussy,' he grated drily. 'Now all I need to know is how cheap are you?' There was nothing low-cost about the sum he went on to mention.

Sabrina could hardly believe her ears, or his crudity. The audacity of the man to try and buy her off as if she were some... some... Words simply failed her and all she could do was stare at him in outrage.

For some reason he seemed to take her silence as some sort of bargaining technique and immediately he raised the price.

Sabrina leaned back into her chair and drummed her fingertips against the smooth leather. Boy, was this man going to have to do some apologising when Garth told him the truth! The mere thought was enough to lighten her mood and it brought a gleam to her eyes. 'So what's the deal? I take the money and run far away from London like a good little girl?'

'On that kind of money you can run where the hell you want, just as long as it's well away from Garth Fraiser,' he answered drily.

Sabrina gritted her teeth and tried to imagine him grovelling at her feet for forgiveness tomorrow. That would be sweet revenge indeed. Yes, Garth would have to tell him the truth tomorrow whether he had told Nadine or not. She glanced up and met those hard, implacable eyes. Well, maybe he wouldn't grovel, but he would have to apologise. You couldn't insult a woman the way he had and then just forget about it, especially when the woman in question was a relative—albeit a distant one. Her mouth curved in a bitter smile. Garth would be furious when he heard what his stepson had accused him of.

'Sorry, but I will have to turn down your kind offer.' She forced a light airiness into her tone now. 'I'm far too happy with my life here to give it up for mere money.'

He looked at her as if she had just sprouted two horns. 'You are not going to try and tell me that you are in love with Garth, are you?' The deep voice was scornful. 'You don't think that he will leave his wife for you, do you? The only thing that you can offer is an enticing little body, something that can be picked up anywhere. Garth is not about to sacrifice his marriage for that.'

Sabrina literally flinched at those cutting words. It was strange just how much they hurt. She should just ignore his words, ignore him. But his contempt for her stung bitterly. 'You don't know me, Mr Kingsley, but I can assure you that I have a lot to offer in any kind of relationship,' she told him with quiet dignity. There was a vulnerable light in her blue eyes for just a moment before she turned them away from him, her dark lashes flickering down.

For a little while there was silence between them and Sabrina sensed that her words had thrown him off balance a little.

'Why don't you just leave now?' she asked coolly.

'I want you to consider my offer.' His voice was grim. 'It is a very generous one, considering the fact that if Nadine finds out about you you will be out of Garth's life so quickly your feet won't touch the ground.'

'Is that supposed to be a threat?' Her head jerked up angrily.

'You had better believe it.' The dark eyes sliced over her slim figure once more before he turned towards the door. 'You've got twenty-four hours.'

Sabrina sat and stared at the door for a few moments after he had gone. Only when she heard the powerful engine of his car firing into life did she climb stiffly to her feet to move towards the phone.

She had every intention of ringing Garth immediately until she noticed what time it was. It was hardly fair to bother him with all this at eleven o'clock at night, and she couldn't really ring him at home in case Nadine answered the phone. It would be better to wait until tomorrow and she could ring him at his office.

She replaced the telephone receiver with a sigh and, switching off all the lights, went up to bed.

Of course, she couldn't sleep. Marc's dreadful accusations kept playing and replaying in her mind. Then she found herself remembering how she had responded to his caresses only a few days ago and her face felt as if it was on fire.

It had all been a game... the way he had kissed her, the way his hands had run over her body, the invitation to Paris. All the time he had hated and despised her, and been trying to win her around so that he could get her out of his stepfather's life.

At that moment she hated Marc Kingsley more than she had ever hated any man. She would make him pay for the way he had treated her. One way or another she would make sure that Marc Kingsley was very, very sorry for this.

CHAPTER FIVE

THE first thing that Sabrina did the following morning was ring Garth's office. She was told by his secretary that Mr Fraiser would be out of his office all day.

'Has he left a number where he can be reached? It is important,' she asked, feeling her nerves twisting at the thought of spending another night like last night.

'I'm sorry. Ring again on Monday morning.'

With a frown Sabrina thanked her and put the phone down. 'Damn,' she spoke aloud as she glared at the of-fending instrument. What on earth was she to do now? Ring him at home? She still had his number from the days when she had worked for him. But what if Nadine answered? Would she think it was strange that Garth's ex-secretary should phone him?

She could always ring and pretend to be someone else, but that just seemed ridiculous. She paced up and down thinking about it. She didn't want to give Nadine any cause for concern, and maybe if Marc thought that she was having an affair with Garth Nadine might suspect something too. She raked a trembling hand through her hair. This was awful.

In the end she had to content herself with the thought that she would be seeing Garth tomorrow anyway. They had arranged to go out for lunch to celebrate her birthday, and Garth was picking her up at midday.

Even though she kept herself busy, that day seemed interminable. She drove over to her mother's house in

Richmond and made a start at cleaning it from top to bottom.

Clearing out that house was a sad task. Her mind wandered continually to her mother and happier times. Then she thought about Marc Kingsley's accusations and could have wept...it was all such a mess. Had Garth really bought her flat at Kensington for her?

It was her mother who had brought home the details of the apartment. She had said that a work colleague who had moved abroad was selling it and would she be interested? Of course she had been interested. The property had been in beautiful condition and a mere snip. She had moved in soon after her twenty-first birthday. For a moment her eyes frosted with tears. Had the apartment been a twenty-first birthday gift from a father she had not known?

Garth had cared about her. He cared about her now. She went home looking forward to seeing him the next day. It was her twenty-sixth birthday, a time to start over, a time to get to know her father. Garth would put everything right; he would sort out Marc and that would be the end of her problems with him.

Despite the stern pep talk she had given herself, Marc tormented her thoughts throughout that night. She kept thinking about how charming he had seemed...how happy she had felt just at the touch of his hand against hers. She kept remembering the way she had responded to his kisses and she felt like dying of shame. She tried to rationalise her behaviour by telling herself that he had caught her at an emotional low.

Yes...that was the answer. She had been at a vulnerable point of her life. She was still in trauma over the loss of her mother, over Garth, and he had taken advantage of that. In ordinary circumstances she would never have responded to Marc Kingsley like that . . . he wasn't even her type, she finished furiously as she buried her head in her pillows and prayed for the oblivion of sleep.

She was up very early the next morning. There were a few birthday cards for her in the early morning post. One was from Garth wishing her happiness and love. She smiled as she placed it in pride of place on her mantelpiece and then went to shower and change.

She chose a turquoise-blue suit from her wardrobe. It was an outfit that suited her tremendously well. It highlighted the blue of her eyes, the red-gold tones in her hair. Satisfied that she looked her best, she went downstairs to wait for her father's arrival.

Twelve o'clock came and went. Garth did not arrive. By one-thirty Sabrina was pacing up and down. Had Marc somehow stopped her father from coming? She dismissed that thought impatiently. Marc didn't know Garth was taking her out, and anyway how could he stop Garth from coming? Even Marc Kingsley wasn't that powerful.

Maybe Garth had forgotten it was her birthday today? But then he had remembered to send her a card. By three o'clock she was frantic. It just wasn't like Garth to be late; he was a very punctual man. She was in half a mind to try ringing him at home, but then his wife might answer and what would she say to her? When it was nearing four o'clock she decided to drive over to his house. Maybe she would see his car in his drive . . . anything to put her mind at rest.

Traffic was heavy going out of London, and she was slowed to almost a standstill at one point. Her nerves felt frazzled and she reached for the radio, hoping to find some soothing music. Instead she caught the summary of the four o'clock news.

The name Garth Fraiser caught her attention and she turned the volume up, thinking it would be about some bill he was heading at Westminster.

'The accident happened at eleven this morning on the westbound carriageway. No other vehicle was involved and the police say they don't know what caused the accident. Mr Fraiser is in a critical condition at Charing Cross Hospital.'

Sabrina's heart seemed to stand still as she listened to that news. Her hands froze on the wheel, her mind clouded with panic.

Garth was in hospital! He could be dead or dying while she had been idly waiting at home. Wildly she glanced up, looking for the road signs that would lead her to Charing Cross. The impatient hooting of some cars alerted her to the fact that she had just switched lanes in a rather careless manner. Desperately she tried to calm down before she also had an accident.

It seemed to take forever to reach Charing Cross Hospital and even longer to find some parking. She locked her red Volkswagen with trembling hands and hurried towards the hospital's main entrance.

The strong smell of antiseptic assailed her nostrils as she walked along the corridors, her heels tapping on the tiled floors as she approached the desk that she had been referred to from the main desk. As the young nurse looked up at her, she could feel her heart thudding so wildly that it was an actual pain in her chest.

'I'd like to know how Garth Fraiser is, please.' With an effort she found her voice. Suddenly she was remembering her mother's death. The full horror of it was still so fresh. She had been notified of the accident while she had been at work. Garth had brought her to the hospital but she had been too late; her mother had already died.

'Mr Fraiser is still in Intensive Care,' the girl answered her after a moment's consultation with a list in front of her. 'His condition is critical. Are you a relative?' The nurse's eyes narrowed on the pallor of her face.

Sabrina hesitated and then shook her head, biting down on the softness of her lower lip. 'Is there any chance that I might be able to see him for just a few moments?' she pleaded.

'I'm sorry, only immediate family are allowed in.' The answer was brisk. 'We will contact them when there is any change.'

But who will contact me? Sabrina wondered frantically. Who will tell me if my father is alive or dead? 'Couldn't I just see him for one minute?' Her eyes were wide and beseeching.

'I'm sorry. As I have said, it is close relatives only. Mr Fraiser is still unconscious.' The nurse moved away from her, busying herself with some files that were sitting on a counter behind.

Sabrina watched with a feeling of utter helplessness. I am a relative, she wanted to scream. I'm his daughter. But the words only echoed around inside her, making her feel more desolate and alone than she had felt in a long, long time.

A heavy hand on her shoulder made her jump nervously. She turned and looked up at the dark, penetrating eyes that never failed to throw her off balance.

'What the hell do you think you are doing here?' Marc Kingsley demanded in a low, furious tone.

He was dressed in dark cords and a black polo-neck jumper that managed to make him look even more austere and forbidding than usual. He loomed over her, his eyes sweeping over the pallor of her skin, the fear in her expressive blue eyes.

'Well?' His voice was granite-hard.

'I'm waiting to see Garth. I want to know how he is.' The defiant tone of her voice was a little shaky.

'My God, but you've got some nerve.' He raked an angry hand through his thick dark hair. Before he could continue, however, they were interrupted by a rather breathless voice beside them.

'Mr Kingsley, could you tell us how Mr Fraiser is doing?'

Sabrina turned to see a dark-haired young woman and behind her a man with a large TV camera over his shoulder, and a couple of other reporters.

She heard Marc's muttered oath before he turned to face them.

'He is still on the critical list,' he told them briskly.

'And could you tell us who the woman was that he was on his way to visit?' The questions continued quickly. 'We believe that he was taking her a large bouquet of red roses with a note attached that read——'

'Yes, all right,' Marc cut in impatiently. 'I know what was on the card...as I suppose the whole of England will tomorrow. What news station are you with?'

Sabrina was hardly listening now as the implications of the reporter's words hit her. Garth had actually been on his way to her when the accident had happened. Distress and remorse flooded her entire being. If only she had turned down his invitation to lunch. Maybe then

Garth wouldn't have had this terrible accident . . . it was all her fault.

She was only vaguely aware of the strong arm that Marc was placing around her waist. It was only when he drew her closer in against his body that she looked up.

'I know exactly what was written on that card for the simple reason that I was with my stepfather when he wrote it,' Marc was saying now.

She stared up at him feeling totally bemused. What was he saying? That card must have been a birthday greeting from Garth. Had Marc really been with him when he had written it? Had Garth therefore told him the truth?

'It read, "To my darling girl with all my love." ' There was a fiery warmth in the dark eyes that stared down at her, an undercurrent of emotion in the deep velvet voice that could have been mistaken for tenderness by the people watching, but not by Sabrina. She could hear the unleashed fury behind his words, see the menacing shadow in his eyes that was so cleverly hidden away from the lenses of the cameras that were trained on them.

'It was his birthday greeting to the woman I love,' Marc continued smoothly. 'You see, I had just told my stepfather that I intend to marry Sabrina Harrington and he was highly delighted as he knows Sabrina well and is fond of her. She used to be his secretary.'

Sabrina's mind was reeling with shock. What was he saying? Why was he telling these reporters such lies?

'He was on his way to see my fiancée when the accident occurred.'

The reporters seemed to be lapping up the story. One with a camera rushed forward to take their picture.

'How long have you known each other? When is the wedding to take place?' All kinds of questions were hurled at them after that. Marc fielded them all with an ease that frankly bemused Sabrina and at the same time he steered her through them and out towards the exit.

Once outside in the cool air he turned to face them again as they followed him outside. 'If you wouldn't mind, we would like to be alone. As you can probably appreciate, we are both very upset.'

'Upset' was putting it mildly. Sabrina was shaking with reaction, both to the onslaught of the Press and the fear that Garth might die.

'Where have you parked your car?' Marc muttered in a furious undertone as he led her away from the rabble of reporters.

'I... I don't know.' She shook her head, desperately trying to collect her thoughts. 'Over there somewhere.' She waved a hand vaguely in the direction she thought she had come.

He glared at her. 'You're in no bloody fit condition to drive,' he grated under his breath as his eyes took in her distress. 'Come on, I'll put you in a taxi.'

'No.' She stopped walking. 'No, Marc, I want to stay here. I want to know how Garth is.' She was nearly crying; she felt hysterical. All she could think of was that she didn't want to lose her father the way she had lost her mother. Life couldn't be so cruel, not when she had just started to pick up the threads of her life again, had just started to know her father.

'Look, you little fool, you're making a scene.' Marc glanced sharply over his shoulder to see if the reporters were still watching. 'You can't stay around here. Don't you care anything about Garth's reputation?'

She stared blankly at the harsh, attractive features. At that moment she cared about nothing except Garth's recovery.

With a muffled oath he turned her around towards him. She stared up at him, aware that he was too close yet unable to do anything about it. His hand moved up to lace his fingers through her soft, silky hair in a gesture that managed to look amorous when in fact it was downright aggressive. He held her forcibly still, while his lips invaded hers with a cool, brutal passion that made her gasp. It could only have lasted a minute, over before it started really, but it sent all of Sabrina's senses reeling into complete chaos.

Then he smiled coolly at her. 'Let's just hope that has satisfied our audience.' His arm went around her shoulders like a hard band of steel as he turned her to walk with him again.

'You are going home,' he muttered to her as they moved, 'even if I have to tie you up and gag you to get you there.'

She was too breathless, too bemused to argue.

He lengthened his strides so that she was practically running to keep up with him. It was almost a relief when he stopped next to his car and unlocked it.

'Get in,' he ordered curtly as he opened the door.

Something about that tone made her snap out of the daze she had fallen into. She glared at him, her eyes mutinous. 'I don't want to go anywhere with you.' Her heart was pounding, her lips still burning from the way he had kissed her a moment ago. She was livid with anger.

'Don't you think that you have done a good enough job trying to ruin Garth's reputation as it is without drawing any more attention to yourself?' he grated harshly. He steered her none too gently down towards the seat of the car and she could feel her anger crumble.

She got in without a murmur, those condemnatory words sapping her energy. She was too tired to argue with him.

Marc didn't speak one word as he manoeuvred the car through busy traffic back towards Kensington.

It was rush-hour now, everything in creation seemed to be on the roads, and it was starting to rain. Sabrina watched the windscreen-wipers going backwards and forwards with a swishing sound, her mind seeming to go back and forward with them. One moment she was thinking about her mother, the next about Garth.

Surely Garth wouldn't die; surely fate couldn't be so cruel. If only she hadn't agreed to having lunch with him ... if only ...

She pushed her hair back with a hand that was none too steady and turned to look at the stern profile of the man next to her. 'Do you think Garth will be all right?'

He shrugged. 'I don't know.' His voice was hard, with no gentle edge, no trying to soothe her nerves.

'You think that I am to blame for Garth's accident, don't you?' Her voice was no more than a husky whisper, but she knew that he had heard her despite the fact that he didn't make any immediate reply. 'If it weren't for me Garth would have been at home with his wife and none of this would have happened ... that's what you're thinking, isn't it?'

He slanted a derisory glance in her direction. 'It is a little late for contrition,' he stated drily. He reached behind him and took out some newspapers that were lying on top of a briefcase, and without ceremony dumped them on to her knee. 'I suppose you have seen these?'

Sabrina stared down at the evening newspapers with wide, stricken eyes. Each paper carried the story of Garth Fraiser's accident on the front pages along with the question, 'Who is Garth Fraiser's darling girl?'

'Sensationalised trash,' Sabrina muttered furiously.

'The words were written on a gift tag attached to some red roses,' Marc grated drily. 'Apart from making a laughing-stock of a well-respected man, you have probably done untold damage to his career. Not to mention the hurt you could inflict on Nadine.'

'Nadine hasn't seen these, has she?' Sabrina's face went from pale to ashen.

'No... she was at a charity lunch when the accident happened. She went straight to the hospital and has been there ever since.'

'Thank heavens for that.' Sabrina shuddered with relief.

'Don't bother to act like the concerned little innocent,' he snapped. 'I know you couldn't give a damn about Nadine.'

She frowned. 'You are wrong, Marc. I do care.'

'Oh, yes, you care so much that you could hardly wait for her to leave the country before meeting her husband.'

'That's not true!' She glared at him.

He slanted a glance at her. 'Come on, as soon as you heard that she was in Nice you were around at her house, arms firmly around her husband,' he grated with bitter contempt. 'I know the truth, remember? I know that the real reason you turned down my invitation to come to Paris is because you have designs on Garth Fraiser.'

'You don't know anything,' she murmured icily.

'Oh, I know your type,' Marc said harshly. 'An opportunist, out for what you can get from a man that you think you can twist around your little finger.'

'That's a lie.' Sabrina glared out of the passenger window, her eyes blurring with tears. 'You don't know me at all.'

Sabrina tried desperately to get her emotions back under control. She shouldn't allow Marc Kingsley's accusations to upset her so much. They were wrong; he didn't know the truth.

'You shouldn't have told those lies back at the hospital,' she said suddenly as she remembered what he had told those reporters. 'You had no right to——'

'I have every right to try and protect Garth's interests,' he cut across her angrily. 'Those reporters are not stupid. They know Nadine and Garth have not been spending much time together recently. Naturally they would have continued to dig to see who those red roses were for. Hopefully they won't bother now.' He slanted a derisory glance at her. 'Your turning up at the hospital didn't exactly help the situation. You had a damn nerve.'

'I was worried about him,' she said in a tight, strained voice. 'And I didn't know about the flowers or the note.'

'Worried about your meal ticket, more like.' Marc pulled the car up outside her apartment.

About to argue with him, Sabrina suddenly changed her mind. What was the use? Marc Kingsley was obviously determined to think the worst of her and unless she told him the truth he would never believe anything she said. Should she tell him the truth? The question burned inside her.

Silently she got out of the car and was surprised when he also got out and followed her up to her front door.

She turned to face him. 'Shouldn't you be getting back to the hospital?'

'Not until we've talked,' he said calmly.

'I have nothing to say to you.'

'Well, I have plenty to say to you.' He took her front-door key from her hand, opened the door and walked in, leaving her no alternative but to follow him.

'Cup of tea?' he asked nonchalantly as he headed straight into her kitchen.

'No, I do not want a cup of tea. This is utterly ridiculous,' she spluttered indignantly. 'You wanted to talk to me, so talk.'

'OK.' He took out one of the kitchen chairs and sat himself down.

For just a moment Sabrina was forcibly reminded of the night when he had brought her home and made the coffee. She had thought him quite kind, had felt very attracted to him. Those thoughts seemed so foolish now as she looked into the dark fury of his eyes.

'You realise of course that the papers will be full of our engagement tomorrow?'

She held his gaze with difficulty. 'So it seems. What are you going to do about it?'

'Do about it?' he drawled in a jeering voice. 'What do you think I'm going to do about it? I'm going to play at being the loving fiancé for a couple of weeks until the storm has passed, and you are going to go along with it.'

'What?' She stared at him as if he were speaking another language. 'I hardly think this is necessary.'

'Of course it's damn well necessary,' he exploded angrily. 'I would have thought that was fairly obvious... even to a bimbo like you,' he jeered. 'You and

I are going to do a little PR exercise to take any whisper of scandal away from my stepfather.'

'Now I know you are crazy,' she murmured with a shake of her head. 'I can't believe that you are actually contemplating going along with that absurd story you spouted to those reporters.'

'Why else do you think I spouted it?' he asked drily. 'It was the only thing I could think of at the time to save the situation.'

'It won't work . . . it's madness. We hardly know each other, for heaven's sake . . . it's not even credible.'

He gave her a dry look. 'It was a whirlwind romance.' He got to his feet and paced up and down the kitchen. 'Love at first sight,' he muttered sardonically.

'Ha, ha, very funny.' She put one hand on her hip. 'No one in their right mind is going to believe that. It will be patently obvious to anyone who has eyes in their head that we can't stand the sight of each other.'

'We'll see.' He slanted a look around at her. 'You managed to gaze into my eyes with considerable effect in Paris, when you were weighing up how much you could get out of me.'

Her face burned at his words. 'I wasn't weighing up anything,' she said stiffly.

'No?' One eyebrow lifted mockingly. 'I think you were. I think you wondered if I would be a more lucrative proposition than my stepfather. Then when you got back to London you decided Garth would be infinitely easier to manage. He falls hook, line and sinker for those shimmering tearful eyes, doesn't he?'

'Don't be ridiculous!' Her voice trembled with rage. For just a moment she was filled with a violent urge to fling herself at him and pummel against his arrogant face with clenched fists. 'And I couldn't look at you now with anything other than contempt.'

'Knowing what wonderful acting abilities you have, I'm sure that's not true.' His lips twisted in an arrogant way. 'You managed to simulate such passion in my bedroom in Paris. I'm sure if there is enough at stake you could do it again.'

'I hate you, Marc Kingsley.' She ground the words out fiercely, meaning every syllable.

He looked completely unconcerned. 'And does that hatred stretch to Garth as well?' he asked smoothly.

'Of course not.' Her eyes clouded as she thought of Garth...dear, dear Garth.

'Cut the theatricals, for heaven's sake,' he drawled out contemptuously. 'If you give one damn about Garth Fraiser you will start looking at me with devoted admiration. Otherwise the man you claim to care about so passionately will end up without a career and maybe even without a wife. You know what the papers are like once they get a sniff of a story—they want to blow it out of all proportion.'

For a moment those words struck a chord in Sabrina's heart. He was right. The papers would try to make something of it, as Garth was a well-known personality. Would it be better to tell the truth...surely the truth was always the better option? Should she tell Marc?

'Of course, maybe it would suit you if he ended up without a wife,' Marc continued derisively. 'Although you might not be so keen on him if he loses his job.'

'I'm not having an affair with Garth Fraiser,' she said in a shaking voice. 'I want you to believe that.'

'I'm sure you do.' He sounded amused for a moment.

She pushed a hand through her hair. She didn't know what to do. Garth had asked her not to say anything. She had promised him that she wouldn't, but this was intolerable.

A frown marred her face. 'How long are you contemplating keeping up this ridiculous pretence?'

'For as long as it takes.' His eyes raked over her in an arrogant way. 'Don't worry, I'm as eager to see the back of you as you are of me. I certainly don't want to prolong the agony. In a few weeks we will have a very public argument and the engagement will be off.'

She bristled furiously at his manner. 'I hope you know that Garth is going to be furious when he hears about this.'

'Garth will be relieved that I have managed to smooth things over,' Marc assured her without hesitation. 'His political career means a hell of a lot to him and, if word of this scandal ever got out, he would probably end up having to kiss it goodbye.'

Sabrina fell silent. For all she disliked Marc she knew he was right. If people thought that Garth Fraiser was having an affair it could do untold damage. But he wasn't having an affair, she tried to reason with herself. Surely the truth should be told...surely the truth wouldn't hurt his marriage or his career? Then why hadn't Garth spoken out about it from the beginning? a small voice whispered inside her. Obviously Garth hadn't been sure what effect the truth would have, and if he wasn't sure could she in all conscience speak out now?

She sighed and twisted her hands in an unconscious nervous gesture. The whole thing was such a mess ... she felt totally confused and so alone. She glanced over at

Marc. 'What exactly did they say about Garth's condition at the hospital?' she asked him bleakly.

'Only what I told the Press.' He glanced at his watch. 'I'll have to be getting back there. I want Nadine to go home and lie down.'

Sabrina swallowed hard. 'Did they give out any hope that he would regain consciousness?'

'They didn't say much, probably because they don't know much at this stage.'

She closed her eyes for a moment. They felt so heavy and tired, as if lead weights were attached to her lashes, and there was a sick feeling in the pit of her stomach that just wouldn't go away.

'When you have finished playing the grief-stricken lover, Sabrina, perhaps we could talk terms?' He cut into her thoughts in a cruel sardonic tone.

'Terms?' Her eyes flew open, wondering what on earth he was talking about now.

'I thought that would get your attention.' He came closer to her.

Sabrina watched the tall, powerful figure with a feeling of doom. Marc Kingsley made her feel like a frightened impala running from a lion. Running and running yet knowing that he was closing in on her, knowing it was only a matter of time before he sprang for the jugular vein.

'Shall we say the same amount that we mentioned before?' The quietly asked question made her jump nervously.

'I don't know what you are talking about; I——'

'Come, come, Sabrina, there is no need to be coy. I mean, of course, the second figure I named. The one with the extra zero at the end.' His eyes raked over her

pale features. 'I realise that you will want ample re-
muneration for acting as my fiancée.'

For a moment she almost laughed aloud. He was offering to pay her to act out this crazy charade. The man
thought that she was totally without principle—a mercenary, scheming woman. She shook her head. 'I don't
want your damn money.'

He came even closer, a menacing look on his dark
features. 'I won't go any higher. That is my price. In
exchange you will play the part of my adoring fiancée
in public and then disappear when and how I tell you.'
His voice was clipped and precise, like an army major
giving out his instructions. It was obvious that he was
taking her compliance as a matter of fact. In Marc
Kingsley's eyes all that mattered to her was money, and
he was sure that his offer was so lucrative she wouldn't
be able to refuse.

She shook her head and her eyes glittered furiously.
For two pins she could have hit him. He was the most
awful, the most arrogant, obnoxious... Words failed
her. 'I'm afraid, Mr Kingsley, that you are wasting your
time...' About to reject the whole crazy idea and send
him on his way with a few choice words, Sabrina was
suddenly struck by a thought.

If she angrily threw him out, how would she know
how Garth was? She was going to have to rely on him
for news of her father. No one would phone her if there
was any change in his condition. She would be relegated
to watching the newspapers for news of him. For a
moment the torturous image of sitting alone at her
apartment not knowing how Garth was made her ani-
mosity towards Marc Kingsley die. 'I don't want your

money, Mr Kingsley,' she said quietly, 'but I will go along with your little game . . . for a few days anyway.'

He gave a short derisive laugh. 'So you are a bit of a gambler as well as an actress.'

'I beg your pardon?' Her blue eyes gleamed with distaste as they watched the cynical curve of his lips.

'Well, obviously you are hoping that Garth will recover and you can carry on as before.' His crisp voice was like a whiplash in the room. 'So of course you will turn down my offer of money when there is still the slightest chance that Garth will come through for you with so much more.'

'I've had enough of your disgusting accusations, Marc Kingsley.' Her face flushed with furious heat, her eyes burning into his. 'Yes, I care if Garth gets better, but it's not for any mercenary reasons. I happen to love him . . . I suppose that is hard for someone like you to understand, but it happens to be the truth.' She spoke passionately and without thinking. It was only when she finished that she wondered about the advisability of that last statement.

A chilling silence descended on the room. The look on Marc's face made her heart race with fear.

'Well, at least you're no longer trying to tell me that you're just Garth's secretary,' he murmured icily. 'But I doubt very much if you know what love is.'

Anything Sabrina might have said to that last statement was swept to one side as he continued in an imperious tone, 'So you had better give me a spare front-door key.'

'I beg your pardon?' Her voice was as cold as his.

'I'm supposed to be your fiancé . . . remember?' he grated drily. 'If it's to look convincing then I'm going to have to spend some time around here. You had better make up a spare bed for me.'

'I will do no such thing,' she blazed furiously.

'You will do exactly as you are told.' He reached out a hand and tipped her chin up so that he could stare down into her eyes. 'If I were in love with you, then I would be around here sharing your bed.'

Her mouth seemed to go dry with panic, her heart thudding even louder in her ears.

'We will have to make things look realistic, won't we?' He spoke as if to a child. 'Now give me a key and I will see you later on tonight when I come back from the hospital.'

Trembling, Sabrina pulled away from him.

'You know it makes sense,' he said as he held out his hand for the key. 'Besides, this way I will be able to keep you up to date with Garth's condition.'

She stared at him, not knowing what to do.

'Come on, Sabrina, I haven't got all night. I want to see what's happening at the hospital and talk with Garth's doctors.'

She nodded slowly. 'All right.' She turned to get her handbag. She didn't seem to have much choice but to just go along with this ... for the time being anyway ...

With a frown she handed him her spare set of keys. 'Do you intend to come back here after talking with the doctors?'

He shrugged. 'I don't know.' He turned and headed for the door. 'Don't wait up for me. Just leave my bedroom door open so I know which it is.' He glanced back at her with a mocking smile. 'I wouldn't like to get the wrong room.'

'Don't worry, I would soon put you right,' she assured him in a freezing tone.

'Would you?' The question lingered in the air as he left without another word.

She glared at the closed door, hating Marc Kingsley more than she had ever hated anyone.

CHAPTER SIX

SABRINA did sit up waiting for Marc that night. Not because she wanted to see him, but because she was so anxious to know what the doctors had said about Garth.

She drank cup after cup of coffee and sat in front of the television in case there was an update on the news about Garth.

It was a shock to see herself on the news. The pictures that had been taken at the hospital of her and Marc were on each bulletin.

'Millionaire Marc Kingsley was very much in love with the mystery girl that Garth Fraiser had been on his way to visit.' They kept saying it, over and over. The same pictures, the same spiel. Nothing different about Garth's condition.

The awful thing was that she and Marc did look in love on the TV. It was frightening how the truth could be completely distorted and still look convincing when you heard it on the national news.

They showed a fleeting glimpse of Nadine arriving at the hospital. Sabrina's heart went out to the poor woman. She must be going through hell. They also said that Garth's daughter Madeline was flying home from America to be at her father's bedside.

All Garth's family were gathered around him, all except her. Guilt mingled with tears inside her. She should be with him; it was all her fault.

She found herself remembering how good he had been to her when her mother died. The way he had tried to protect her and help her.

At one o'clock she switched off the television and went to bed. Obviously Marc wasn't coming back here to-night. She left the spare-bedroom door open just in case he did return. Contrary to his little joke, she did not want him coming into her room by mistake. The mere thought of it appalled her.

She had a bath before going to bed, more to relax her stiff, aching muscles than anything else. Usually she found a hot bath soothing, but tonight she just couldn't relax. She slipped between cool sheets and closed her eyes but sleep refused to come.

It was nearing three when she heard the front door open. Instantly she was alert. She heard him cross the hallway and make his way down the corridor. Quickly she got out of bed and reached for her dressing-gown. She had to know how Garth was. This not knowing was driving her mad.

When she opened her bedroom door he had already closed his. With a frown she hesitated, then, taking her courage in both hands, she crossed and knocked on his door.

He opened it almost immediately. His eyes, moving over her pale, anxious face, held a moment's concern. 'Are you all right? You don't look too well.'

For just a second his solicitude startled her... then she realised that he was probably just bothered in case she was backing out of their arrangement. 'I just wanted to know what the doctors said.' With an effort of will she didn't snap at him; she knew that if she did he probably wouldn't tell her anything.

'Come in.' He stood back to allow her into the bedroom. She hesitated, suddenly unsure. She didn't want to go into the room.

'Come on, come on, I'm not going to bite,' he muttered impatiently and turned away. He was in the process of hanging some clothes in the wardrobe from a suitcase. He continued with the job as she reluctantly came further in.

'So what did they say?' Her voice sounded husky with apprehension.

He hung the last shirt up and turned to look at her. 'He's in a coma.' His voice was so grim and yet so matter-of-fact that she just stared at him for a moment in silence.

'But he's going to be all right?' Her breath seemed to catch in her throat as she asked the question.

He shrugged. 'They don't know; it's looking pretty bad.'

'Oh, God.' She could feel her face crumpling and she turned blindly away from him, not wanting him to know that she was crying.

'For heaven's sake, girl.' His voice was very brusque. 'You are taking this acting too far.'

She made no reply, just hurried from the room and closed her own bedroom door behind her with a certain feeling of relief. Only when she climbed back into bed did she allow the tears to flow freely. She sobbed silently into her pillows, her heart filled with grief and with prayers.

She must have drifted into an exhausted sleep, because the next thing she was aware of was the sound of music coming from the lounge. She blinked and sat up. It was early, almost seven. Quickly she got out of bed and reached for a pair of jeans and bright blue mohair jumper. She glanced briefly at her reflection in the mirror before leaving the room. What she saw did not please her. Her eyes looked swollen, her face grey. Impatiently she went into the bathroom and bathed her face. It didn't look much better for her efforts, but with a sigh she left her room. She didn't care what she looked like anyway.

It was the television that she could hear. Breakfast TV was playing to an empty lounge. She went through to the kitchen and found Marc sitting at the table eating some toast. The smell of freshly ground coffee hung in the air.

'Good morning.' Marc glanced at her thoughtfully, his eyes lingering on her swollen face. 'Would you care for a coffee?'

About to tell him that this was her kitchen and she would get her own coffee, she changed her mind. She was too tired to argue and anyway she never seemed to win when she exchanged angry words with him.

'Thanks.' She sat down in the chair opposite him and watched as he got to his feet and found her a cup and saucer, then poured her a black coffee.

Again memories of the first evening she had met him surfaced to taunt her. Then, close behind, the memories of Paris...of that kiss.

'Did you sleep at all?' he asked abruptly as he sat down opposite her again.

With a supreme effort Sabrina pulled herself together. She didn't bother to lie. 'A few hours.' She sipped the drink gratefully. 'Are you going back to the hospital now?'

He nodded. 'I want Nadine to get some rest; she's been there all night. But somehow I don't know if I'll get her to leave. She can be very stubborn.'

Like her son, Sabrina wanted to say, but she bit her tongue on that. 'I'm sure you will talk her around.'

She glanced over at him, an unconsciously pleading light in her eyes as she added in a low voice, 'Do you think I could see him? I'd only stay a few moments; I just want——'

'No,' he cut across her, his voice firm and unequivocal. 'You have no right to be at that hospital.'

She glared at him, her blue eyes sparkling with intense dislike now. 'You are a very callous man, Mr Kingsley,' she told him in a brittle voice.

He shrugged, not in the slightest bit moved by her opinion of him, and finished eating his toast.

'Why can't I see him?' She couldn't let the subject drop without trying a little harder. 'I can't see any harm in it.'

'Well, luckily I can,' he said drily. 'My mother has enough to worry about and Madeline will be arriving today. The answer is no; don't ask me again.' He got up to put his empty plate in the dishwasher, then poured himself another coffee.

Her fingers clenched tightly around her cup as she watched him. It was pointless trying to appeal to the man's better nature; there seemed to be no softness in him, no sensitivity. Obviously she would never get around Marc Kingsley. If it was up to him, she would never see Garth again.

'And don't call me Mr Kingsley,' he said abruptly as he sat back down. 'I've told you to call me Marc. So you may as well get used to it. I don't want you making any blunders when we are in company.'

She didn't make any reply, just watched him with eyes that spoke volumes. For a moment the injustice of it all stung bitterly. Madeline could sit by her father's bed...but she couldn't. Madeline could hold her father's hand, could tell him she loved him—— She cut her thoughts off, annoyed by her self-pity. Thinking like that didn't help anything.

'You'll have to put all that acting ability to its best use this afternoon,' he continued wryly. 'Nadine wants to see you.' His lips twisted drily. 'She wants to tell you how happy she is about our engagement.'

'Oh!' Nerves fluttered inside her. She didn't like the idea at all. Lying to total strangers was hard enough, but deceiving Garth's wife seemed totally appalling.

'So you will have to be on your best behaviour. Leave most of the talking to me,' he advised her sardonically.

'I'll be happy to,' she said stonily. 'You are probably much more adept at lying than I am.'

He gave her a narrow-eyed look. 'Your sanctimonious comments are wasted on me, Sabrina. For your information I will do whatever is necessary to save my mother further heartache. If that means telling a few lies for a couple of weeks, so be it.'

Sabrina finished her coffee, her mind working overtime. She wished that she could tell Nadine the truth, but she was afraid of causing Garth problems. She would never forgive herself if she was the cause of their marriage breaking up.

'So I think we should get our facts straight,' Marc continued briskly. 'We met first when I called into Garth's office and there you were. I was attracted to you immediately.'

Sabrina frowned. 'But I never saw you at Garth's office.'

'Well, I know that and you know that, but Nadine doesn't, does she?' he drawled mockingly. 'It will make it sound more realistic if we say we met a while ago. That we were attracted to each other immediately.'

She made a face. Somewhere deep inside she was determined to let him know that she had never felt attracted to him. 'It sounds laughable to me.'

'I didn't see you again until a week ago when we bumped into each other outside Garth's offices,' Marc continued as if she hadn't spoken. 'I realised when I saw you that I didn't want to let you escape out of my life. That I wanted you. I took you out to Paris and proposed to you at my house. If we stick as close to truth as possible we won't forget what we have said.'

'Oh, please!' Sabrina groaned mockingly. 'I feel totally nauseated.'

He gave her a cold stare. 'This is important, Sabrina. Make a mistake and you'll regret it, I can assure you of that.'

She didn't like the threatening note in his voice. It sent a wave of apprehension racing through her. It would not be wise to cross Marc Kingsley, she knew that as she held those dark eyes for a moment.

'I told Garth all about it yesterday morning. He was highly delighted and was coming to see you when the accident happened,' he finished in a no-nonsense tone. 'Have you got that?'

'It's not the most romantic story that I've ever heard,' she said drily, trying her utmost not to let him know that he was unnerving her.

'Well, I suppose you prefer your romance a little more illicit,' he grated in a raw tone.

She didn't dignify that comment with an answer, just glared at him. 'My car is still at the hospital. Will you give me a lift on your way so that I can pick it up?' she asked instead, trying to keep to practical conversation.

'All right.' He glanced at his watch. 'Are you ready to go?'

'Yes.' She picked up her bag from the counter behind her, checking that her keys were in it.

'OK.' He stood up. 'I'll just get my jacket from the hall.'

Sabrina went through to the lounge to switch off the TV. She was just in time to catch a feature on Marc...'one of Britain's most eligible bachelors, who announced yesterday that he is planning to get married'. They then flashed up a picture of a very beautiful dark-haired girl.

'Imogen Müller, whose name has been closely linked with Marc Kingsley, had no comment to make about Marc's engagement to Sabrina Harrington as she flew into London late last night.'

For just a moment Sabrina's heart thudded most peculiarly against her chest. Marc had a serious girl-friend! A girlfriend who looked devastated, if the picture on the television was anything to go by.

'Well, she can have him,' Sabrina muttered to the attractive blonde presenter, with a note of sarcastic venom in her voice. 'You can have him as well.' Then she switched the television off with a decisive finger as they started to show the pictures taken yesterday at the hospital. Turning, she found Marc watching her with some amusement.

'Very generous, Sabrina, but she is not my type.'

'I thought anything in a short skirt would be your type,' Sabrina muttered, not quite daring to look him in the eye as she insulted him. 'And who is Imogen Müller?'

'Why, darling, you sound jealous,' he said in a sardonic tone.

'Don't flatter yourself,' she grated huskily. 'I'm just asking so that I don't look a complete fool if someone mentions her.'

'I see.' Marc put his jacket on as he spoke. 'There's really nothing to tell. She is twenty-two, vivacious, beautiful and daughter of a German multimillionaire who I'm doing some business with.'

'I see.' For some reason Marc's description of Ms Imogen Müller really irritated Sabrina. 'I hope your whirlwind engagement to me doesn't affect your business.' She drawled the words in a sarcastic tone, a gleam in her blue eyes that told him very clearly she hoped that was the case. 'Daddy might be angry if you've hurt his little girl.'

Marc shrugged broad shoulders. 'I'll take my chances. Roland Müller is no fool; he knows a good deal when he sees one.'

Sabrina gave him a small tight smile. 'Well, if you feel like taking Imogen Müller out, don't worry about me...I shall not be making any objections.'

'What? Now that I'm an engaged man?' Marc's voice was as sarcastic as hers had been. 'Darling, surely you know I have eyes for no one but you now.'

'I'm starting to feel nauseated again,' she said, making a face as she walked towards him.

'As long as it's not morning sickness, I don't give a damn how you feel,' he said drily as he put a hand on her shoulder. 'So don't feel free to get involved with anyone else for the next few weeks.'

She stopped in her tracks, her face flooding with colour, her heart drumming against her ribs with painful anger. Just what kind of a woman did he take her for? 'How dare you say something like that?' She lifted a hand and, catching him off guard, caught him a stinging blow to the side of his face.

After she had done it, she was so shocked by the red hand mark along his cheek that she could only stare at it in horror. The act of slapping him seemed to have released the pent-up boiling anger inside her and now she just felt depressed. 'I—I shouldn't have done that...' she stammered, lifting her eyes to his. 'I'm sorry.'

For a moment she thought he was going to punish her in some way. His dark eyes narrowed to mere slits and his mouth took on a hard, cruel line. In that instant she was really frightened of him.

He lifted a hand to his cheek and then to her surprise he shrugged. 'I shouldn't have said what I did. I'm the one who should be apologising.'

She was so stunned that she couldn't say anything. Was the almighty arrogant Marc Kingsley really apologising?

'We are both very wound up. I think we should try and refrain from making digs at each other,' he said as he turned to leave. 'This situation is hard enough.'

Tears misted her eyes. Her emotions were up and down like a see-saw. The only thing keeping her together was her anger towards this man, she realised grimly. She didn't want him to start being nice to her. That would be the last straw.

They travelled to the hospital in silence. Marc was angry with her. She could tell by the grim set of his mouth and the way he was changing gears in the car, but he kept his thoughts to himself.

When he parked the car he looked over at her, his eyes travelling over her pale features contemplatively. What was he thinking? She would have given anything to be able to read those stern eyes.

'Can you remember where you parked your car?' The solicitous question surprised her.

She nodded. 'Yes, thank you.'

'OK.' He got out of the car and she followed him. 'I'll try and persuade my mother to come back with me to your house at about lunchtime. She just might agree if she thinks you are expecting her.'

'Sabrina nodded dumbly. 'Do you want me to make lunch?' Heavens, this was a strange conversation after the intense insults of before.

He shook his head. 'Just tea and biscuits. We won't stay long. I'll take her home to lie down after that.'

Sabrina nodded. She was walking with him towards the hospital entrance. 'Where is your car?' he grated suddenly.

'Back there.' She waved a hand idly behind her. 'I just want to know how Garth is before I leave.'

'Oh, no.' He came to an abrupt halt. 'You are not coming in.'

'Says who?' Sabrina glared at him like a mutinous child. 'I have every right to go in there.'

The conversation might have blown into another full-scale row, only someone shouting Marc's name interrupted them.

They turned to see a pretty brunette hurrying towards them. She was about twenty years of age and dressed very stylishly in a pale pink suit that did wonderful things for her curvaceous body.

For a moment Sabrina thought it was Imogen Müller and her heartbeats increased dramatically and painfully. She didn't want it to be Marc's girlfriend; she couldn't cope with it.

'It's Madeline,' Marc said in a low tone. 'Just watch what the hell you say.'

For a moment Sabrina's breath froze inside her. Madeline Fraiser was her half-sister. Coming unexpectedly face to face with her was a shock to the system.

'Marc...oh, Marc.' The girl broke down as she went into Marc's outstretched arms. 'It's so awful about Dad...how is he?'

'He's holding his own, sweetheart.' Marc stroked her hair tenderly, then smiled gently down at her. 'It's good to see you again...even if it is in these difficult circumstances.'

Sabrina couldn't help comparing Marc's comforting, gentle manner with the way he had been speaking to her recently. Lucky Madeline, she found herself thinking. Marc is obviously very protective of his half-sister.

Madeline looked up and tried very hard to smile at him. 'What's all this about you being engaged? I read something on the plane about someone called Sabrina...is it true?'

'Certainly is,' Marc said calmly. 'She's right behind you.'

'Oh...' Obviously Madeline had only had eyes for Marc because she was totally surprised to find Sabrina standing behind her. She turned, and for the first time Sabrina found herself looking into her half-sister's eyes.

Her first thought was that although Madeline was dark like her mother and Marc she had the same vivid blue eyes as she did.

'Hello, Madeline,' Sabrina said in a husky tone.

The next moment she was being embraced in a warm bear-like hug. 'I'm so pleased,' the girl whispered as she pulled away to look at Sabrina. 'I hope you know that you're getting the best catch of the century.' She tried to laugh through her tears, obviously doing her best to put on a brave face when all she could really think about right now was her father.

'Next to Dad, Marc is the kindest and most lovable man in the world,' Madeline continued softly.

Sabrina tried not to let herself look at Marc as she sought to formulate a reply to that. 'Yes . . . I know,' she managed to say in a low tone.

'Of course she knows,' Marc put in with a grin.

'And you are very lucky, Marc—Sabrina's beautiful,' Madeline continued quickly. 'It will be lovely to have a sister.'

Oh, the bitter irony of it, Sabrina thought with a wretched feeling deep inside her. All she wanted to do was tell the truth and have everything out in the open.

Marc, glancing down at her, frowned as he caught the expression on her face. 'Darling, I think you should be going now,' he said in a low tone.

It took one or two moments for Sabrina to realise that he was talking to her.

'Goodbye, Sabrina,' Marc said again in a voice that held a subtle note of warning.

'All right,' Sabrina nodded. It was probably best that she go, before she said something she might regret.

'You're not staying?' Madeline looked a little surprised.

'Sabrina has to leave,' Marc said firmly. 'You will see her later. Meanwhile let's go in and see how things are with Garth.'

Madeline nodded. 'How's Mother taking it all?'

'Badly—she's been sitting by his bedside all night.' Marc put an arm around his sister. 'Come on, let's go and try and persuade her to take a break.' He glanced over at Sabrina. 'I'll see you later,' he said pointedly.

Sabrina watched them disappear into the hospital, their arms tightly around each other. In that moment she felt like an intruder. Marc was right. She had no right to be here. She was intruding on Nadine's grief. She didn't belong at Garth's bedside.

She turned and made her way back towards her car. It started to rain, a heavy April shower slanting through watery sunshine. Sabrina picked up her footsteps; she had forgotten her coat and the rain was soaking through her woollen jumper.

Wet and miserable, she finally reached her car. Numbly she started it and headed back towards Kensington. She was dreading Nadine's visit this afternoon. Lying to Madeline had been bad enough, but to have to face Garth's wife and tell her she was madly in love with her son was intolerable. Her heart thudded uncomfortably at the thought.

When she got home she had to shower, and changed into a pair of black ski-pants and a black and white tunic top. Her hands shook as she dried her hair.

She thought about the awful argument with Marc that morning, and then found herself wondering about Imogen Müller. Was Marc serious about her?

She stared at her reflection in the mirror. Why on earth was she even wasting time thinking about Marc and Imogen Müller? She couldn't give a damn...all she cared about was Garth getting better.

With a sigh she went into the kitchen and started to load the dishwasher with the breakfast things. It was a relief to keep busy; she didn't want to think about facing Nadine.

At twelve she started to prepare some lunch. She wasn't hungry and she knew Marc had said not to bother for his mother. Yet she felt she should prepare something. Nadine should eat to keep her strength up.

She made a lasagne, and then worried that maybe Nadine wouldn't like Italian food.

At one o'clock on the dot she heard Marc's key in the front door. 'Sabrina, where are you?' he called from the hallway.

'Coming.' With her heart in her mouth she rushed out into the hallway. Marc was alone.

'Where's Nadine?' Now that she found she wasn't here, perversely Sabrina felt disappointed.

'Wild horses wouldn't drag her away from Garth.' He raked a tired hand through his hair. 'She sends her apologies and says that she is looking forward to seeing you soon.'

Sabrina nodded. She understood Nadine's reluctance to leave her husband. 'How's Garth?'

'The same.' He frowned. 'There's a nice smell in here.'

'I made some lunch.' She shrugged, feeling self-conscious for some reason. 'I . . . I know you said not to, but I thought Nadine should eat something.'

Marc looked at her strangely. 'I see.'

Sabrina doubted that he did. He was probably trying to work out some ulterior motive for her cooking lunch for who he thought was her lover's wife.

'Are you hungry? It seems a shame to waste it,' she said coolly.

'Yes, I am actually.' Marc took off his jacket and followed her into the dining-room.

He stopped as he noticed the beautifully laid table. 'You've been busy.'

'It was something to do instead of worrying about Garth,' she answered him truthfully, and then flushed as his dark gaze raked sharply over her.

'I'll just get the food. Sit down.' Hurriedly she escaped into the kitchen.

She took a moment to compose herself before going back inside with the lasagne.

'Is Madeline still at the hospital with Nadine?' Sabrina asked as she served him a generous helping.

'Yes. They are talking to him, in the hope that he can hear them.'

Sabrina swallowed hard on the sudden knot in her throat. The thought of Garth just lying there made her insides twist.

'This is very good.' Marc glanced across to where she was sitting, just toying with her food. 'Aren't you going to eat anything?'

'I'm not really hungry.' She reached instead for her glass of water.

She noticed that he had stopped eating and was watching her through narrowed eyes.

'What's the matter?' she asked nervously, then as a sudden ridiculous thought hit her she laughed rather mirthlessly. 'The lunch isn't poisoned, if that's what you're thinking. I'm not desperate to get rid of Nadine, no matter what you think.'

He grinned at that. 'Actually I wasn't thinking that.'

'Oh?' She tried not to care what he was thinking. But after a moment's silence she had to ask.

He smiled at the question. 'I was wondering if you had any plans for this afternoon?'

'Why?' She looked over at him suspiciously.

'I thought I would take you to buy a ring.'

'A ring?' She stared at him incredulously.

'I do believe that is the custom between an engaged couple,' he replied laconically.

'I think you're taking this engaged thing too far.' She shook her head. 'I don't want a ring. Anyway it's Sunday; the shops will be closed.'

'So they will.' He said nothing more, just finished his lunch and then sat back.

As she started to clear the dishes away he got up to help her.

'It's all right. I can manage, thank you,' she snapped icily when their hands touched accidentally as they both reached for the bowl of salad.

He smiled. 'All right. In that case, can I use your phone?'

'I suppose so.' She went back into the kitchen. His polite tone was grating on her tender nerves. At this moment she honestly thought she preferred him when he was snapping at her.

She emerged from the kitchen a little while later to find him relaxing on the settee in the lounge.

'Are you going back to the hospital now?' she asked him nervously. She really didn't want him around her for too long.

One dark eyebrow rose. 'Anyone would think that you were trying to get rid of your darling fiancé.'

'Would they?' she answered him in the same mocking tone.

'And no, I'm not going back to the hospital, not for another few hours anyway. I'm taking you for a drive.'

'I don't want to go for a drive,' she snapped. Why on earth should they go for a damn drive? she wondered angrily. Was it some kind of publicity stunt?

'Nonsense.' He stood up and his dark eyes were serious now. 'Of course you do.' His tone held a rather stern warning.

She glared at him. 'I gather I don't get a choice in this?'

'Correct.' His tone was brisk. She knew there was no way she was going to win. If she refused again he would probably lift her bodily from the room.

'I'll get my coat.'

She went upstairs and got her coat from the wardrobe. She caught her reflection in the dressing-table mirror and sighed. She looked so pale and washed out, the strain of the last couple of days clearly evident. She pulled a brush through her hair so that it sat neatly around her shoulders and then brightened herself up with some lipstick. Feeling a little better, she joined Marc who was waiting in the hall.

His eyes flicked over her face and her slender figure with a gleam of male appreciation that was not lost on

Sabrina. Suddenly she felt nervous again. This whole situation had got out of hand.

'Where are we going, anyway?' she asked him, a defiant look on her face.

'It's a surprise.'

She glowered at his back as he turned to open the door. He really was a most infuriating man.

As she settled herself in the comfortable seat of his car, she told herself that she didn't care where they were going. She was past caring.

Once more the journey passed in near silence. Once or twice she flicked a nervous glance at him, wondering what he was up to now.

He caught one of those glances and smiled. 'You don't need to look so worried. I'm not taking you to have all your teeth extracted.'

She looked sharply away from him. She hated him to know that she felt nervous; it left her feeling at a distinct disadvantage. 'I'm not worried,' she declared staunchly and then, as if to prove her point, she struck up a conversation.

'What did Nadine say when she heard you were engaged?'

'Surprisingly it brightened her up. She thinks you're a lovely girl.' He flicked a derisive glance at her and she was annoyed to feel her skin grow hot.

'She wants to see you,' Marc continued briskly. 'I'll try to arrange something for tomorrow. Can you remember the details of our courtship in case she asks you?'

'As if it was yesterday,' she said drily.

The car sped along roads that were quiet compared with the usual weekday traffic.

'Where did I propose to you?' He snapped the question at her, reminding her for a moment of one of her old schoolteachers—one that she hadn't liked very much at that.

With a sigh she went along with his questions in a bored tone.

'And what did you think when you first saw me?' he continued crisply.

Her eyes flew towards him. 'We didn't rehearse that bit.'

'You've got an imagination, haven't you? Use it,' he grated sardonically.

She thought for a moment. 'I thought you were an arrogant swine,' she said truthfully.

To her surprise he laughed at that. 'Yes, my mother would believe it. You can use that.'

'Your mother has no illusions about you, then, has she?' Sabrina said with a wry grin.

'She thinks I'm the most wonderful thing on God's earth, actually,' he said with a gleam of amusement in his voice. 'As do most women.'

'Except me,' she said briskly, and then some gleam of devilment prompted her to add, 'And maybe Imogen Müller now.'

Silence greeted that statement and she wondered if she had caught a raw nerve as she glanced at his handsome features. Maybe he was upset about losing Imogen? It was strange, but she felt a brief flash of pain at that thought. What on earth was the matter with her? she wondered grimly. Her emotions were in smithereens.

It was hard to tell just what state Marc Kingsley's emotions were in. As always he looked cool and composed as he pulled into a car park and manoeuvred the

Porsche expertly into a space. Only when he had switched off the engine did he make a reply.

'I don't know what Imogen thinks. I haven't spoken to her yet,' he said seriously. 'It would hardly be fitting.'

'Would it not?' She hated his smug, superior attitude. And she hated the way he had carefully placed the word 'yet' into his sentence as if he would be picking up with Imogen Müller at any time. Nothing seemed to throw Marc Kingsley off balance.

'Perhaps I should ring my boyfriend and tell him to pay no attention to the newspapers...that I will be picking up with him again soon.' She didn't know why she said that...she didn't even have a boyfriend. She was just filled with an incredible urge to let Marc see that she wasn't at all interested in him; that she had her own romantic life and it had nothing to do with Garth.

'That will be a bit difficult, won't it? Seeing as your only boyfriend is lying critically ill in hospital.'

'Garth is not my boyfriend.' Her voice rose unsteadily.

'But you love him anyway?' Marc's voice was abrasive. 'Save it, Sabrina...I know all about you. The guy I employed to investigate you told me you had a casual boyfriend called Steve for just a couple of months last year; that you finished with him just before your mother died.'

She could only stare at him open-mouthed. 'My God, you tried very hard to dig under every conceivable stone, didn't you?' she lashed out furiously. She couldn't believe that he even knew about her ex-boyfriends. 'So tell me, how does Steve fit into your accusation that I've been having an affair with Garth for years?' she asked bitterly.

'Simple. You were two-timing him. I'm sure you're very good at that.'

She shook her head and her hands clenched into tight fists of anger.

He merely smiled. 'Watch your temper, Sabrina. Remember what we said this morning.' Then calmly he got out of the car, leaving her fuming silently.

He came around and opened her door for her, leaving her no option but to get out or cause a scene. She got out.

'Where are we going?' she snapped in an irate tone.

'A little spot of shopping.' He linked her arm as if they were the best of friends. 'Now remember,' he said in a low voice, 'we are supposed to be in love, so hold on to me and smile up at me with adoration at every opportunity.'

'What a load of rubbish,' she muttered angrily. 'Even if I were in love with you I wouldn't behave like that. We are not a couple of teenagers, for heaven's sake.'

'You've obviously never been in love,' he said drily.

She fell silent at that. It was true—she had never been in love. Oh, she had had boyfriends but not one of them had stirred any great depth of emotion in her. Sometimes she had longed to find that special someone. Someone who would take her in his arms and keep her cherished. Someone who would be her best friend as well as her lover. It was a hard combination to find. Most men were only interested in her body, not her mind.

They walked through the busy streets. As it was Sunday only a few of the shops were open. Marc stopped outside a very prestigious jewellers and rang the doorbell.

'They're closed,' Sabrina said, flicking a puzzled glance up at him.

'Not to me, they're not.'

Sure enough the door swung open and a middle-aged man smiled a welcome at Marc. 'Hello, Mr Kingsley, nice to see you again.'

The door opened wide to them and they stepped inside. 'I hope we haven't kept you waiting,' Marc said politely. 'It's very good of you to open the shop for us.'

'It's no problem.' The man led them through to a back room that was luxuriously decorated in red and gold. 'Please sit down.' He waved them towards two Louis XIV chairs and flicked on the bright overhead lights.

'Now, let me get some cases out for you.' He unlocked some cabinets behind him and brought out several trays to put them on the table in front of Sabrina. 'There you are; now take your time. Perhaps I can get you both a coffee?'

'Thanks, Dave, that would be nice.'

Sabrina was barely listening to the exchange of words; she was too busy staring at the trays of diamonds and rubies, emeralds and sapphires. The rings were fabulous. They sparkled so brilliantly under the lights that she was dazzled by them.

'So what do you think, darling; which one takes your fancy?' Marc asked her lazily.

Sabrina looked up as the man discreetly left them to get their coffee. 'I don't want any of these,' she hissed in a low voice.

'Why not?' For a moment he looked at her as if she had just said something sacrilegious.

'Because... because they must be worth a fortune and we are not really engaged.' Her whisper became louder as she became more and more agitated. 'If you have to buy me something, buy me a cubic zircon.'

He laughed at that with genuine amusement. 'My dear Sabrina, sometimes you are very entertaining.'

'Believe me, that isn't my intention,' she muttered angrily. 'I just think you are going too far.'

'And you're worried that when Garth comes out of his coma he will be less than amused by your wearing a ring that looks in any way serious?' he enquired smoothly.

'No, I just don't want an expensive ring.' She tried very hard to keep her temper.

His lips curved into a lop-sided smile. 'I'm sorry, Sabrina, but I do have my reputation to think of. If I put a cubic zircon on your finger, shares in my companies would probably slump overnight—it could cause a major panic on the stock-market.'

'Now who's being amusing?' she grated drily.

He shrugged. 'You would be surprised. People notice things, and a rumour can do untold damage once it gets going.'

'Here we are.' The owner of the shop returned with a tray of coffee. 'Have you seen anything you like yet?' he asked Sabrina with a beaming smile.

She fought down the impulse to ask to see some costume jewellery. There was a part of her that wouldn't have minded starting a rumour... any kind of rumour if it would hurt Marc Kingsley.

Instead she picked up the largest diamond ring on the tray and slipped it on her finger. It fitted perfectly. 'I don't know,' she murmured reflectively as she held up her slender hand so that the diamond glinted with red and blue fire.

'That, if I may say, is the most beautiful ring among the selection,' the man said hurriedly. 'It is a flawless diamond.'

'Really?' Sabrina held it up towards Marc. 'What do you think, darling?' she asked huskily and looked up at him with wide, innocent blue eyes. She knew full well that the ring was worth a small fortune and she had no intention of choosing it, but she hoped to give Marc Kingsley a nasty turn. He was infuriating her and he damned well deserved to have that smug smile wiped off his face.

He shrugged and looked completely unconcerned. 'Do you like it?'

'It's very nice.' She flashed it backwards and forwards, admiring the rich warmth of the colours flashing from it.

'Right, then, we'll have that one,' Marc said nonchalantly to the man who was waiting with a rather hopeful expression on his face.

'Er...no.' Sabrina started to try and take it off, horrified that he was really going to purchase such a ring.

'Keep it on, darling.' Marc leaned across towards her and, catching her unawares, kissed her briefly on the lips. 'The most beautiful woman deserves the most beautiful ring,' he murmured in a husky tone as he looked into her blue eyes.

For a moment her heart skipped a beat. The warm, seductive tone and the feeling of his lips against hers gave her the strangest feeling in the pit of her stomach. She couldn't find her voice to make any further protest, and by the time she had Marc was already following the man through to the other room to settle the account.

'Well, you're very quiet,' Marc said to her as they walked back to the car a few moments later.

She shook her head. She was still dazed with the speed of what had just happened and she could hardly believe the ring that sparkled so beautifully on her left hand. 'You shouldn't have bought such an expensive ring,' she murmured finally, not knowing what else to say.

He laughed drily. 'I'll have to hand it to you, Sabrina Harrington, you are good. You actually sound like a girl who hasn't a mercenary bone in her body, a beautiful young innocent.' He flicked her an amused glance. 'Sometimes I'm not at all surprised that Garth was taken in by you.'

Sabrina made no answer to that. She felt surprisingly upset by the incident and his cutting remarks. She wasn't mercenary. She hadn't really wanted him to buy her that ring. She had only been trying to wind him up and now it seemed the joke had been a big mistake.

He opened the door of his car for her. 'Don't look so worried, my darling,' he drawled with lazy amusement. 'I'm sure you will repay me a thousandfold for the ring.'

Sabrina didn't like the suggestion in those words. She darted a very worried glance into his dark eyes. He didn't mean he wanted payment in kind—did he? She had the most awful feeling that her little joke had just backfired in a very big way.

CHAPTER SEVEN

NOTHING much was said as they drove back to Kensington. Marc dropped her outside her apartment but didn't get out of the car.

'I'm heading back to the hospital now,' he said briskly. 'I might see you later on tonight.'

A tremor ran through her body at those words, but she said nothing.

She let herself into the house and then watched from the safety of her curtains as he pulled out into the traffic once more. She didn't understand Marc Kingsley. Why had he just spent such an astronomical amount of money buying her a ring? And that crack about her paying him in kind; surely he hadn't meant that?

The ringing of the telephone broke into her thoughts and she turned to pick up the receiver.

'Hello, is that Sabrina?'

She knew immediately that it was Nadine. Her lilting French accent was unmistakable.

'Yes... hello, Mrs Fraiser.' She hesitated nervously. 'How is your husband?'

'He's the same.' She could hear the tense worry in the woman's tone. 'I'm still at the hospital. I've been trying to ring you for a few hours now.'

'Marc took me out... he bought me an engagement ring.' Maybe she shouldn't have told her that? Sabrina stumbled nervously to a halt.

'Oh, my dear, I'm so pleased for you both.' There was no mistaking the genuine warmth in the woman's voice now.

Sabrina felt like a fraud; guilt flooded through her. 'You...you've just missed Marc. He is on his way back to the hospital,' she stumbled nervously.

'It was you I wanted to talk to. I just wanted to apologise for not coming to see you with Marc this afternoon. I know you were expecting me. I just couldn't bear to leave the hospital.'

'It's all right, Mrs Fraiser. I understand, really I do.'

'You must call me Nadine,' the woman insisted. 'After all, you are part of the family now. Hopefully it won't be long before Garth makes a complete recovery and we can celebrate your engagement properly.'

'Yes, yes, that would be lovely,' Sabrina said, a husky tone in her voice.

'In the meantime if you would like to come to the hospital with Marc at any time you must not think you will be in the way.'

Sabrina was totally startled by the invitation.

'Marc told me that you don't like to intrude and I do realise it's not the most cheerful of places,' Nadine continued briskly, 'but I just want you to know that if you wanted to pop down with Marc I would love to see you.'

'Thank you, Nadine.' Sabrina hesitated; she so much wanted to visit Garth yet there was a part of her that was afraid of Marc's reaction if she went in to see him. 'Perhaps I'll come with Marc in the morning,' she ventured cautiously.

'Oh, that would be lovely.' Immediately she was taken up on it. 'I'll have to go now. See you tomorrow.'

Marc was going to be livid, Sabrina thought as she put down the receiver. But to hell with Marc... she was going to see her father.

It was surprising how much more cheerful she felt after that telephone conversation. Nadine had sounded so confident that Garth would get better. She had to believe that she was right.

She spent a busy afternoon then, sorting through some of her mother's clothes for a charity. It was a horrible job and one she found extremely upsetting.

Every now and then her ring caught her attention as she worked. It caught the light in a magnificent sparkle of clarity and beauty, causing her to catch her breath. It was by far the most beautiful ring she had ever seen. For a moment she found herself wondering what her mother would think of this situation with Marc. Would she have advised her to tell him the truth about Garth? The truth could be so damaging... yet maybe it would be safe with Marc?

She didn't know what she should do. Garth had trusted her not to say anything, but circumstances had changed. Would he blame her now?

With a sigh she finished what she was doing and made herself some tea. The apartment seemed so quiet. Only the ticking of the grandfather clock in the hallway broke the heavy sound of silence. She put the television on, but there was nothing she wanted to watch. Finally she went upstairs, had a bath and went to bed. She was totally exhausted, her mind racing in circles. Yet sleep was slow in coming.

She heard the front door closing much later. Sleepily she heard footsteps in the corridor. She waited for them to pass by her room with a kind of breathless feeling.

When the knock came on her bedroom door she jumped violently with nerves.

'Sabrina, are you awake?'

Her heart thudding, she sat up. Was there some news about Garth?

'Yes.' She was in the process of getting out of bed when he walked into the room.

'Do you mind?' Her eyes blazed with anger as she fumbled for her dressing-gown. 'I could have been undressed or anything.'

His eyes moved over her slender figure in the ice-pink flimsy satin nightdress. It had tiny shoe-string straps and just a delicate trim of frothy lace that covered her breasts. His gaze was totally unnerving and she felt herself flushing as she finally managed to cover herself with the matching pink dressing-gown.

'I have seen a woman's body before,' he replied with a dry edge to his tone.

'I'm sure you have.' She stood up. 'But you haven't seen mine.'

There was a second's silence, a second when Sabrina could have bitten out her tongue. Marc's eyes glinted sardonically. 'We could rectify that ... if you want?'

'I don't find that remark amusing,' she said primly.

'And I don't find you arranging to visit Garth behind my back amusing,' he grated suddenly.

So that was what had brought him charging in here. She shook her head. 'Your mother asked me to come down to the hospital.'

'And you jumped at the chance.' His lips twisted with derision. 'I thought I made myself clear when I told you that I didn't want you anywhere near Garth.'

'For heaven's sake, Marc,' she burst out impatiently. 'The man is dangerously ill in hospital. I'm not going in to seduce him.'

'I don't care what your motives are. I told you I don't want you there.' His dark eyes glittered dangerously.

She shrugged. 'Well, Nadine is expecting me. What are you going to tell her?'

'I'll think of something. You are not going.'

Sabrina felt the prickle of tears behind her blue eyes. She shrugged and tried to look as if she didn't care...but she did care and it showed all too clearly on her face.

'Don't look at me like that,' he grated roughly. 'It will get you nowhere.'

'Just leave me alone.' She sat back on the bed and he turned for the door.

'Oh, for heaven's sake!' He turned with exasperation as he heard her sniff. 'Are you going to cry all night again?'

'What do you mean, again?' She glowered at him, irritated beyond words.

'I mean the way you did last night,' he answered calmly.

'I didn't cry last night.' She didn't know why, but she always seemed to end up lying to him.

'Your face always looks swollen when you get up, I take it?' he grated sardonically.

'I'm allergic to having you in the apartment,' she muttered furiously. How dared he point out so rudely that she had looked a mess this morning?

He laughed, but it wasn't a dry, mirthless sound. In actual fact it was warm and genuinely pleasing to the ear.

'You're really very amusing.' He fell silent and watched her for a moment—the vulnerable light in her blue eyes, the slender, very beautiful curves of her body. 'All right,' he said abruptly as if she had just press-ganged him into something. 'I give in. You can see Garth for fifteen minutes tomorrow. Fifteen minutes,' he said quickly as she opened her mouth. 'That's it, no longer.' Then he left her staring open-mouthed at the door.

Why had he changed his mind? She just couldn't fathom Marc at all. With a sigh of relief she got back into bed. But sleep was elusive. Instead she found herself thinking about Marc. She remembered his anger and then his laughter. She remembered the look on his face as he had slid that engagement ring on to her finger. And suddenly she started to cry again.

Why on earth was she crying? Impatiently she brushed a hand across her face. She was going to see Garth tomorrow... and he would get better soon. Yet the tears still fell. She was crying because of Marc. That knowledge really shook her. Why should that horrible arrogant man have the power to upset her so much? She buried her head in her pillows and with a severe effort of will pulled herself together. After all, she didn't want to look swollen and blotchy when she saw Nadine tomorrow.

The last thing she thought of before falling asleep was Imogen Müller—was Marc in love with the beautiful brunette?

She got up early and showered, then dressed in a blue suit that was both casual and stylish. Her hair sat in a perfect shining thick swath around her shoulders and her face, although still pale, looked better than it had yesterday.

Marc was already in the kitchen. Didn't he bother to go to bed? she wondered grimly. The man seemed to be always up at the crack of dawn.

'You look better this morning,' he remarked lightly as she crossed the room to boil the kettle. 'The allergy seems to be abating.'

She pointedly ignored the remark.

'Am I to take it you're not talking to me?' he asked in a tone that suggested he wasn't in the least bothered.

'Yes, I'm talking to you.' She poured her coffee. 'I just don't think that such a ridiculous statement warranted an answer.' She sat down at the table, and avoided looking directly at him. 'How was Garth yesterday?'

'The same. I would have told you if there had been any change.'

She knew that, but she wanted to keep the conversation strictly away from anything personal, and Garth was the subject that sprang to mind.

She sipped her coffee and then flicked a nervous glance at him. He was so vital-looking. Dynamic, full of confidence and just oozing sex appeal. She shook away the thought crossly. Marc Kingsley didn't appeal to her at all. His good looks were...too obvious.

'Yes?' He caught her staring at him and raised a dark eyebrow.

'Nothing.' She tried very hard not to blush. 'When do you want to set out for the hospital?'

'As soon as you are ready.' He stood up. He was so tall, and his dark business suit made his shoulders look like those of an athlete, not an office worker.

Hurriedly she dragged her eyes away from him, before he saw her staring again. She finished her coffee and stood up. 'I'll just get my bag.'

It was a warmer day than yesterday. Sabrina noticed that the trees were knotted and ready to sprout their rich green colours of spring. She loved the spring, had always thought it was the time for starting over, for fresh new beginnings. For a moment she remembered Paris and the way she had strolled hand in hand with Marc along the banks of the Seine. She remembered the feeling of happiness inside her. That day seemed like an eternity ago. As they pulled up at the hospital, she couldn't help wondering if she would ever feel happy again.

She felt her spirits dampen even more as she walked into the hospital at Marc's side. She remembered how she had dashed in here a couple of days ago. Then she remembered her mother. She prayed that Garth would be all right.

Marc slipped an arm around her shoulder as they approached the same desk where Sabrina had been refused entry to see her father. She knew he had put that arm around her for his mother's benefit, but she didn't shrug him away. Surprisingly it felt reassuring being so close to him. She even felt herself relax against him a little as he opened a door that led through to a private room.

A passing nurse smiled warmly at him. 'Hello, Mr Kingsley.'

'Hello, Sally. You still on duty? You work too hard.'

For some reason Sabrina felt a momentary dart of anger at the easy way he spoke to that nurse. What on earth was the matter with her? she wondered, irritated by her own thoughts.

Garth's room chased all other thoughts out of her head. He was lying very still, tubes coming out of his mouth, a lot of machinery around him. Sabrina felt herself go weak at the knees as she looked at him and she was very glad of that arm around her waist now.

Nadine was sitting by the bedside and she looked around with a smile as they came in.

'Hello, I'm so glad you've come.' Her eyes moved from one to the other and her eyes glimmered with tears for a moment. Then she stood up and came to embrace Sabrina. 'It's so good to see you.'

Immediately Sabrina felt guilty. Would Nadine feel the same if she knew the truth? Lord, she hated this deception.

Nadine Fraiser was an attractive woman in her fifties. She was willowy slim and wore an ice-blue dress that floated around her long, slender legs as she moved. Her dark hair was peppered with silver, and she wore it up in a chignon that gave emphasis to the wonderful bone-structure of her face. Sabrina could see a lot of Marc in his mother. They had the same eyes, the only difference being that Nadine's sparkled with warmth as she looked at Sabrina.

She turned towards the bed. 'Garth, darling, Marc has brought Sabrina to see you,' she said as she crossed closer towards her husband.

Sabrina darted a glance at Marc and he smiled. 'The doctors say we should talk to him. They don't know, he might be able to hear and it could help,' he said in a low tone.

'I see.' She moved closer towards the bed. 'Hello, Garth.' Her voice was slightly husky. 'We all want you to get better soon.'

Nadine smiled at her and pulled out a chair so that she could sit down. 'Marc, would you be an angel and get me a coffee from the machine outside?'

'Certainly. Would you like one, Sabrina?'

She nodded. Her eyes were riveted on Garth's face—he looked so pale, so helpless.

'I've been telling Garth about you and Marc going to get an engagement ring yesterday,' Nadine said cheerfully.

Sabrina somehow managed a smile.

'The thought of a wedding is like a little ray of sunshine in the midst of the gloom,' Nadine murmured.

She looks tired, Sabrina thought as she turned to look at her again. Her heart went out to the other woman; she knew exactly what she was going through.

'May I have a look at your ring?' Nadine asked now with interest.

Sabrina held out a none too steady hand. She felt awful about deceiving Nadine. Obviously she was delighted for them; it seemed cruel to let her believe these lies . . .

'Oh, it's beautiful,' she said breathlessly. 'Perfect.'

'Yes, it certainly is,' Sabrina agreed as she watched how the ring sparkled.

'It's just so romantic,' Nadine murmured. 'A whirlwind love-affair.'

'It was love at first sight,' Marc remarked as he came back in to join them with a tray of coffee.

Sabrina looked up at him and caught the dry glint in his eye. She knew he was referring to the ring.

'We should be having champagne, not coffee,' Nadine said as she took the coffee Marc held out for her.

'There's plenty of time for that when Garth gets out of here,' Marc told her smoothly as he handed Sabrina her drink.

'Yes, we will throw an engagement party for you,' Nadine said at once. 'I know Garth will think it's a marvellous idea. He thinks very highly of you, Sabrina.'

Sabrina avoided meeting Marc's eyes at that statement.

'I was so surprised when Marc told me he was getting engaged.' Nadine looked at Sabrina with a warm gleam in her eyes. 'But when he told me it was to you I could understand his hurry. Garth always said you were not just beautiful, you were a warm-hearted person. He was so upset when you gave in your notice at the office.'

Sabrina felt more uncomfortable by the minute. She could sense Marc's dark eyes boring into her, could sense his disapproval like a tangible force. She tried very hard to forget that he was standing behind her and concentrate on what Nadine was saying.

'So have you set a date yet for the wedding?' Nadine asked as she looked from one of them to the other.

'I think we will wait until Garth is a little better before we go ahead with a date,' Marc said smoothly, then smiled. 'After all, we want him to be able to attend.'

Nadine nodded. 'Yes, that would be nice.' She looked at Sabrina. 'Unless you would rather not wait? I know what it's like to be in love. So I would understand if you want to go ahead and set a date anyway.'

'No, we can wait,' Sabrina said quickly.

Marc smiled down at her and put an affectionate hand on her shoulder. 'After all, we have all the time in the world,' he murmured huskily as he bent to place a kiss on her cheek.

Sabrina tried very hard not to cringe away from him. His closeness completely unnerved her, the touch of his hand and the warmth of his lips on her skin making her face burn with warm colour and her heart jump about like a wild thing.

Nadine looked wistful for a moment as she watched them. 'It's so romantic.' She turned towards Garth. 'I wish you could see these two lovebirds,' she said brightly. 'It would do your heart good.'

'Where's Madeline?' Marc changed the subject as she turned back towards them.

'I sent her home...the poor girl looks exhausted.'

'So do you. You should really go home and try and get some sleep for a while.'

'No, Marc.' She shook her head firmly. 'My place is here. I need to be beside Garth when he opens his eyes.'

The door behind them opened and they were interrupted by a doctor. 'Mrs Fraiser, could I have a word?' he asked quietly.

She stood up immediately. 'Yes, of course.' Putting her coffee down, she turned to leave the room.

Marc went with her out into the corridor, leaving Sabrina alone in the room. She leaned closer to Garth and on impulse reached out to touch his hand that was lying on top of the white sheet.

'Garth, I hope you can hear me,' she said in a low voice. 'It's Sabrina. I...I just want you to know that I love you and——'

'When you are quite finished,' an arid voice interrupted her from behind and she stiffened and let go of Garth's hand abruptly.

'I didn't hear you come back.'

'Obviously.' Marc's face was grim. 'If you are ready I think we will leave.'

She wasn't about to argue with him. One look at his expression had been enough to warn her against that. 'All right.' She stood up. 'Where is Nadine?'

'In the nurses' office.'

'Is everything all right? What are they telling her?'

'To go home and get some rest this afternoon. Without much success.'

'Oh.' Relief flooded her. She had thought for one awful moment that they were telling her something bad about Garth's condition.

Her eyes moved back to her father. 'Goodbye, Garth.' Her voice was low. 'I'll see you soon.'

Marc stood to one side and let her precede him out of the room.

'I should say goodbye to Nadine,' she murmured as they walked down the corridor.

'Such manners—amazing considering you are out to steal her husband,' he grated sardonically.

'I'm not, Marc.' Her eyes shimmered with tears. 'I——'

She was interrupted by Nadine coming out of an office beside them. She looked strained and tired but there was a determined expression in her eyes.

'We are going now, Mother,' Marc said, his tone once more gentle.

She nodded. 'Thank you for coming, Sabrina.'

Marc didn't give her a chance to say anything in reply. 'I'm taking Sabrina with me to my office. She has very kindly offered to do some work for me.'

Sabrina's eyebrows rose at that. She had said no such thing.

'I'll be back around dinnertime. I suppose you will still be here?' he continued briskly.

'Of course. I'm staying here until he gets better.'

'You are a stubborn woman,' Marc said, but there was no malice in his tone. He bent and kissed her cheek. 'See you later. You know where I am if you need me.'

'Why did you tell Nadine that I was going to do some work for you?' Sabrina asked as soon as they were outside.

'Because you are.' He opened the door of his car for her and she got in.

'I seem to recall that there was talk of payment in kind yesterday?' He looked at her rather pointedly as he got behind the steering-wheel.

She stared at him. So that was what he had been talking about when he had bought her that ring.

He saw the surprised look in her eyes and smiled coolly. 'What other form of payment would I want to take?' he enquired silkily.

She felt her cheeks grow hot at the innuendo in those words. She had to admit that when he had made that comment yesterday it had crossed her mind that maybe he had designs on her body. Later she had dismissed the idea as ludicrous. She had told herself he wasn't that kind of man...but what kind of man *was* he?

She shrugged. 'If you wanted me to do some work you should have asked.'

'As I did when I asked you to come to Paris with me?' he retorted smoothly.

'I told you I couldn't move to Paris; I couldn't just up and leave my life here. I have commitments.' She kept her temper with difficulty.

He gave a harsh laugh. 'You need to be committed, you mean. Let's get one thing straight; you have made no commitment to Garth. He is a married man...he won't leave Nadine for you.' He started up the engine of the car and pulled out into the traffic.

Sabrina fell silent. Inside she was seething with indignation. She didn't know what she could say to convince him that she wasn't having an affair with Garth...and she didn't think she could take much more of this.

He pulled into the underground car park of the large Kingsley Enterprises building about half an hour later. They hadn't spoken a word and Sabrina had made up her mind that she wasn't even going to try to be pleasant to him...not when he spoke to her in that awful manner.

They took the lift to the top floor. It opened into a spacious and modern office area where a staff of four girls were working on computers.

'Good morning, Mr Kingsley.' They all greeted him with a smile.

'Morning, girls.' He headed down the corridor and entered an office where a young woman was busy on the phone. 'Oh, Mr Kingsley.' She put the receiver down at once with a guilty look on her face.

'I hope that was a business call,' Marc growled as he strode past her and through into his own office.

'Yes, of course.' The girl sounded breathless with nerves as she hurried after him.

Sabrina had to smile. From the girl's tone of panic she would have placed money on the fact that she had been speaking to her boyfriend.

'Anna, this is Sabrina. She will be helping you out with those foreign reports today.'

From the expression of relief in the young girl's eyes Sabrina guessed that her help was most welcome.

Marc sat down behind his desk. It was an impressive room. The windows behind him gave a sweeping view of the River Thames. The walls were covered with various photographs of his factories around the world.

'Where is my mail? And why haven't you switched the coffee-machine on?' Marc's abrupt voice brought her attention winging back to him.

'Sorry. I left your mail on my desk.'

As Anna hurried through to her own office, Marc rolled his eyes. 'The girl is totally incapable,' he muttered to Sabrina. 'I asked the agency for an experienced secretary to fill in for mine while she's on holiday and they sent me a bumbling idiot of a young girl.'

Anna came back in and placed a stack of mail on his desk. Then she turned to see to the coffee.

'Have there been any calls?' Marc asked her as he started to flick through the envelopes in front of him.

'Yes. Imogen Müller has rung three times. She wants you to call her back. Mr Hoffman has been on the phone and also Mr Anderson.'

Sabrina watched Marc carefully at this piece of information. Did he intend to ring his ex-girlfriend, and if he did, what would he say? Would he tell her the truth—that his engagement was a sham? She bit down on the softness of her lower lip and tried desperately not to mind...but strangely she did.

'OK, get me Hoffman and then give Sabrina those reports we want typing up in French.'

Sabrina followed the girl back into her office and tried very hard to get a grip on her wayward emotions. Honestly, she was cracking up under the strain of everything. She must be going mad to feel upset about Marc talking to Imogen Müller.

'He's not in a very good mood, is he?' Anna said in a low voice as they closed the door between the two offices.

'No, he's not,' Sabrina agreed drolly. At the same time she was wondering why Imogen Müller had rung him three times. She must be very upset.

'How's Mr Fraiser? Do you know?' The girl went across to the phone and then flicked through a book to find a relevant phone number.

'The same.'

'It's dreadful.' The girl dialled the number and when it was answered she flicked the button through to Marc. 'Mr Hoffman for you, sir.'

'I'll get you those reports,' she said then, and crossed the room to the filing cabinets. 'I'm so relieved that you're going to do them. I made a start last week, but Mr Kingsley wasn't pleased with what I did.' She made a face. 'The man is absolutely gorgeous and all the girls in the other offices are mad jealous that I'm in here working for him, but lord, is he a tough boss! He's an absolute perfectionist.'

'Yes, I gathered that,' Sabrina said sympathetically. She took the files that the girl offered her. 'Which desk can I have?' she asked, looking at the two desks that faced each other across the room.

'That one over there.' The girl moved to uncover the electric typewriter for her.

It seemed strange working back in a busy office again. Strange but good. She had forgotten how much she had enjoyed the busy routine, the constant ringing of phones, the cut and thrust of life in the fast lane. By lunchtime she had finished the French report and she had forgotten her anger with Marc.

She was just making a start at helping Anna with sorting out a complicated German document when the door opened and an attractive woman in her early twenties walked in.

It took Sabrina just a moment to realise that this was Imogen Müller, and she was even more attractive than she had looked in her photographs.

She was very slender in a chic black and white Yves Saint Laurent suit. Her dark hair was bolt-straight and sat perfectly in a bob. Under the office lights it gleamed with a healthy mahogany sheen. 'I'd like to see Marc, please,' she told Anna in a rather imperious voice that held just a hint of a German accent.

'Have you an appointment?' Anna crossed to the book on her desk.

'I don't need an appointment, I'm a personal friend. Be good enough to tell him that Imogen is here, please.'

This threw Anna a bit. 'Mmm...I'll check with Mr Kingsley,' she said as she headed for the door through to Marc's office.

Imogen Müller did not look pleased as she waited by the desk. Her eyes drifted momentarily to Sabrina but she did no more than glance at her. Then she frowned and looked back. 'You're not Sabrina Harrington, are you?' The incredulous tone of the woman's voice did nothing to soothe Sabrina's frayed nerves.

'Yes, I am.' She held the girl's gaze steadily. Imogen Müller gave her a hard look, from her gleaming strawberry-blonde hair down to her slender fingers and the ring that sparkled magnificently there.

'You're a stenographer!'

The utter amazement in the woman's voice made Sabrina's temper rise. All right, so she wasn't one of the yuppie set who no doubt were Marc's usual type. But there was nothing wrong with her job and she was very good at it. 'I'm a very highly skilled secretary, if that's what you mean,' she replied coolly.

'Really?' The woman sounded bored. 'Is it true that you and Marc have just got engaged, or is it just a publicity stunt of some kind?'

The abrupt question took Sabrina's breath away. 'Yes, it's true, and it's not a publicity stunt.' The arrogant nerve of the woman made her blood boil. 'Marc and I are very much in love.' Sabrina couldn't have said why she told Imogen Müller that. All of a sudden she had just opened her mouth and the words came out. Maybe it was just because she had wanted to wipe that smug look off the other woman's face, or maybe the reasons ran deeper.

The woman's eyebrows lifted. 'Knowing Marc as I do, I find that hard to believe.'

Sabrina was saved from having to make an answer to that by Marc's arriving in the doorway. 'Imogen, this is a pleasant surprise.'

'Where have you been hiding for the last few days, darling?' Imogen demanded in a coyly flirtatious manner.

'Come through and I'll tell you.' He held open the door for her. 'Anna, dig out the Müller contract, please.' The door closed firmly behind them.

'Hateful woman,' Sabrina muttered under her breath as she tried to concentrate once more on the work in front of her.

'Sabrina?' Marc's voice booming over the intercom on her desk made her jump. 'Will you bring us both in a coffee, please?'

'What's wrong with the coffee-machine in their room?' Sabrina asked Anna, who was frantically searching through the filing cabinet for the contract Marc had asked for.

'I don't know. It mustn't be working.'

With a sigh Sabrina got up and poured two coffees from the machine at the far side of the room. Then, bracing herself to smile, she entered the lion's den with them.

Imogen was sitting in the chair opposite Marc, her legs crossed, showing a very long length of leg in sheer black stockings.

'Thank you.' Marc smiled at Sabrina as she put the coffees down. 'You've met my fiancée, haven't you, Imogen?'

'Yes.' The answer was blunt. Imogen Müller made no attempt to hide her disapproval.

Sabrina turned to leave them.

'I know good secretaries are hard to find, Marc, but really, marrying one is going too far.'

Sabrina heard the insulting remark clearly as she closed the door; what she couldn't hear was Marc's reply. Would he stick up for her, she wondered, or would he just agree with one of his nonchalant smiles?

She returned to her typing with a frown on her face that remained there for the next half-hour while Marc and Imogen were cooped up in the other office.

What on earth were they talking about? Sabrina wondered furiously. She hoped Marc wasn't telling her that their engagement was a sham. It would be too embarrassing after the deliberate lie she had just told.

When they finally emerged Imogen was looking very pleased with herself. 'So, seven-thirty this evening?'

'Seven-thirty,' Marc agreed with a shrug. 'Unless something comes up at the hospital, in which case I will phone you.'

Imogen nodded and then drifted out of the room. She gave Sabrina a triumphant look from cool green eyes as she passed.

He must have told her! Sabrina's heart seemed to plummet like a lead weight into the ocean. Had Imogen told him what she had just said about their being in love? Her mouth went dry with panic and her hands shook. She couldn't even bring herself to look at Marc in case he could see the expression of dismay in her eyes. If Imogen had said anything she would just deny it...she would say she had just been playing her part.

'You can go for lunch now, Anna,' Marc said briskly as he turned back to his office.

Anna reached for her bag and smiled over at Sabrina as the door closed. 'That was Mr Kingsley's ex-girlfriend,' she said in a conspiratorial whisper. 'I think she was a bit upset because Mr Kingsley has got engaged to someone else.'

'Was she?' Sabrina tried not to sound as if she was remotely interested. Obviously Anna didn't realise that she was Marc's fiancée.

'Do you think they were making a date to see each other again?' Anna asked now. 'Miss Müller didn't look nearly as upset when she left. Do you think they have made it up and he's going to finish with his fiancée?'

'No, I don't think so.' Sabrina couldn't help her brusque tone. She didn't want to listen to Anna's idle chatter. She didn't want to discuss Imogen Müller.

'I just wondered. She is very beautiful and Mr Kingsley has got a reputation with the ladies, I believe.'

'He's also engaged to me.' Sabrina's temper was up now. She just wanted the girl to shut up.

The look on the other girl's face would have been funny if Sabrina hadn't suddenly felt sorry for her. She wasn't really angry with Anna; it was Marc who was riling her. Marc who was stirring her emotions in a very strange way. 'It's all right. I know he has a reputation with women,' she said soothingly.

'Oh, I'm sorry.' Anna put a hand to her very flushed cheeks. 'I honestly didn't know. Don't pay any attention to what I've said. I just like to prattle on; a bit of hot gossip lightens the day.'

'It's all right,' Sabrina told her reassuringly.

'I'll go for lunch before I put my foot in it any more.' Anna grabbed her coat and hurried out of the door.

With a grim smile Sabrina turned her attention back to her typing. It was no wonder that Anna thought that Imogen Müller and Marc were reconciled. After all, he had just arranged to meet her tonight and Imogen had looked very smug...like a cat who had stolen the cream. It was intolerable of Marc to make such a blatant arrangement with that woman...he was making her look a real fool.

'Bring that French report in, will you, Sabrina?' Marc interrupted her thoughts through the intercom.

With her mouth set in a firm line she picked up the report and went into his office.

'Thanks.' He didn't even look up at her, just leafed through it with avid interest. 'This is much better. I do appreciate your help.'

'Do you?' Sabrina's voice was sharp.

'Yes.' She had his attention now. 'You can get off when Anna comes back, if you like. I'll get my chauffeur to drop you home.'

'No, thanks, I'd rather get the bus.'

'OK.' He shrugged. 'If that's what you want.'

'It is.'

'What's the matter?' His dark gaze narrowed on her.

'Nothing. Whatever makes you think that something is the matter?' Her voice was blatantly sarcastic. 'Garth is in hospital and I'm engaged to a man who fancies anything in a miniskirt...but there is nothing the matter.'

One dark eyebrow rose at that outburst. 'Do I?'

'Yes, you do,' Sabrina told him heatedly. 'Your reputation precedes you.'

'Who told you that?' he asked calmly.

'It's a well-known fact.'

'And it bothers you to be engaged to a womaniser, does it?'

It struck her suddenly that he was making fun of her. 'I know we're not really engaged,' she said icily, 'but we are supposed to be, and if you continue carrying on with every woman that catches your eye then you can have your damn ring back and the deal is off. I won't be made a fool of by you or any other man.'

'Fine.' His voice was perfectly calm. 'I'll try to concentrate my ardour solely on you, then.'

'I beg your pardon?' She glared at him, her blue eyes sparkling with fury.

'Well, as you have so eloquently spelt out, I am fond of a woman's company.' He shrugged broad shoulders. 'In fact I am missing certain aspects of a woman's company...' He let the words trail in the air with a certain kind of amusement. 'Perhaps I should look to my new fiancée if I can look nowhere else?'

'Try taking a cold shower,' Sabrina advised in a furious voice and then turned to march from the room, Marc's laughter following her.

Sabrina could hardly wait for Anna to come back from lunch. She wanted to leave the office; she wanted to put as great a distance as possible between her and the impossible man she was supposed to be engaged to.

When Anna finally did come back she was almost half an hour late. 'Sorry,' she grimaced as she hurried in. 'I met up with my boyfriend and I lost track of time.'

The door to the main office opened and Marc stood there looking none too thrilled. 'You're late again, Anna.'

'Sorry, Mr Kingsley, I——'

'Come into my office, please,' he cut across her abruptly.

Looking rather worried, Anna hurried to pick up her notebook. Sabrina started to gather her things together for leaving.

'Sabrina, will you come in for a few hours tomorrow morning, please?' Marc's voice halted her as she stood up. 'I just want you to type up another report for me.'

About to tell him to get lost, Sabrina turned and caught the gleam in his eyes. He was enjoying her discomfiture...he was revelling in it. With difficulty she calmed down. Why give him the satisfaction of knowing he was annoying her? 'Yes, if you want.' She picked up her bag and without another look in his direction left the room.

When she got downstairs to the reception area she noticed that it was raining now, and quite heavily. She almost wished for a moment that she had taken up Marc's offer of a ride home. With a sigh she turned up the collar of her coat and went out through the revolving glass doors.

She had just stepped on to the pavement when Marc's black limousine rolled up in front of her and his chauffeur came around to open the door for her.

'Mr Kingsley said you would like a lift home,' he said politely.

For a moment Sabrina hesitated and then with a shrug she climbed into the comfortable vehicle. Why not? It would only seem churlish to refuse now.

As the limousine pulled away from the kerb she glanced up at the impressive Kingsley building and for a moment she imagined that she could see Marc watching her from the window of his office. Watching and smiling, no doubt, because he always managed to have the last word somehow.

CHAPTER EIGHT

MARC didn't come home that night. It was ridiculous to be upset. After all, he hadn't said that he would be sleeping in her spare room every night, just a few nights now and then to make it look as if they were really having an affair. And anyway, Sabrina didn't want him in her house.

So why did she lie awake all night waiting for the sound of his key in the door? Why was her mind filled with tormenting pictures of Marc with Imogen Müller?

Was he with her? she wondered over and over again. He had arranged to meet her tonight, had blatantly arranged the time in front of her. She tossed and turned, angry and then strangely hurt.

As dawn was breaking she had the awful thought that maybe something had happened to Garth and that was why he hadn't come. She gave up trying to sleep then and went down to the kitchen to make herself a drink.

The hours seemed to drag by. She watched the clock with anxious eyes, willing the hands to turn faster so that they would reach a respectable hour for her to ring the hospital. Before that happened, however, she heard the sound of the front door opening.

She flew into the hall, her hands holding tight to the sides of her dressing-gown, so tight that she was nearly tearing the delicate pink material.

'Where the hell have you been?' She launched straight into the attack.

He was still wearing the dark business suit. He looked tired, his hair was slightly ruffled, his face dark with early morning shadow. 'What are you doing up?' he asked, looking startled to see her standing there in her dressing-gown, her eyes blazing.

'I've been worried sick.' She put her hand on her hip. 'I thought something had happened.'

'What, to me?' He looked even more startled now.

'No, to Garth.'

'Ah.' He closed the door as he noticed her starting to tremble.

'So where have you been?' she demanded again.

'Sabrina, you are not my wife,' he said calmly. 'You are not even my fiancée.'

The words had a sobering effect on her. 'Of course not.' Her voice wasn't quite so forceful now. 'I ... I just expected you to come back here last night.' Her eyes burned brightly into his. 'Is Garth all right?'

'Yes, Garth is all right.'

Relief washed through her in great waves. Her eyes moved over him. So where had he been? She didn't dare ask him again. As he had just pointed out to her, she had no right to question him. He looked so tired, weary almost. 'Would you like a drink of tea?' she found herself asking him abruptly.

He nodded. 'Would you bring it into my bedroom for me? I'm going for a shower.'

The request took her by surprise but she nodded and moved through to the kitchen. It didn't take long to boil the kettle and make another pot of tea. Her hand shook slightly as she poured it out and placed it on a tray. Where had he been? The question persisted and niggled. The only answer that kept presenting itself was Imogen Müller.

She went slowly along the corridor towards his room and tapped at the door. There was no answer. She pushed it open slightly and heard the noise of his shower in the *en-suite* bathroom. Cautiously she opened the door further.

'Marc, your tea,' she called as she walked in.

The room was empty, the door to the bathroom slightly ajar.

'Marc, your tea,' she called again, a little louder this time.

He appeared in the doorway. He was naked except for a towel wrapped casually around his waist. For a moment Sabrina couldn't take her eyes off him. She had always known that Marc had a fabulous physique, but seeing him like that brought it forcibly home to her. His chest was powerfully wide and covered in dark hair. The broad shoulders tapered down to lithe hips. She swallowed hard and dragged her eyes away from him with extreme difficulty.

'I'll put it here for you.' She placed the tray beside his bed.

'Thanks. I'm going to try and get an hour's sleep, Sabrina. Could you make sure that you wake me at eight? I must be in the office for nine—I've got an important meeting.'

'Yes . . . yes, of course.' She was starting to sound like an idiot. She moved towards the door.

'Oh, and Sabrina . . .' His voice detained her as she stood with her hand on the door-handle.

'Yes?' She sounded breathless, as if she had been running up and down the stairs all night.

'Thanks for the tea.'

She went back to her own room and lay down on top of her bed. She set the alarm clock to go off in another hour just in case she fell asleep. She needed the sleep, but even though she felt exhausted it refused to come. Had Marc been with Imogen Müller? Why did she seem to care so much?

She remembered how irritated she had been when Marc had spoken in a friendly tone to that pretty nurse at the hospital. She remembered how annoyed she had felt when Anna had pointed out that Marc was a womaniser and could still be having an affair with Imogen Müller.

What was the matter with her? She turned and glared at the early morning light filtering through the curtains. She wasn't a jealous person at all. So why was she jealous about a man she cared nothing about? The answer was such a shock that she sat bolt upright. She couldn't be in love with Marc Kingsley! It was impossible. Marc had said dreadful things to her; he loathed and despised her. How could she possibly love a man like that?

She denied the idea emphatically and lay back down. She didn't want to love Marc Kingsley. He was a womaniser; he was deliberately and calculatingly charming. He was also incredibly good-looking and knew it. It didn't make any sense, then, that she should feel like this about him.

Her heart turned over when she thought about his dark eyes, the way he smiled at her sometimes in a kind of special way. The way he laughed. The way he had kissed her that evening in Paris and made everything inside her melting-warm.

Did love make any sense? Did the rational, intelligent part of her mind not get a say in where her heart chose to love? Marc Kingsley was not the man she would have chosen in a rational frame of mind. She wanted someone tender and warm, someone who cared about her.

The alarm bell rang beside her and she reached out a hand to switch it off. So much for getting some sleep, she thought wryly as she got up. She went across the corridor and tapped on Marc's bedroom door.

'Marc, it's eight o'clock.' There was no answer from the room. She tapped on the door again and pushed it open.

He was fast asleep. He was lying on his back, the white linen covers on the bed only partially covering his naked torso.

'Marc.' She moved further into the room and stood looking down at him.

He didn't make any movement. He looked different in sleep; the tough features were relaxed, gentle instead of arrogant. He had long, very dark eyelashes, she noticed absently.

'Marc.' She moved closer and sat down on the edge of the bed. 'It's eight o'clock.' She placed a gentle hand on his shoulder and he stirred. He opened his eyes and smiled sleepily at her, and her heart seemed to just flip over at the way he was looking at her through those incredibly dark eyes.

'It's time to get up.' She started to get to her feet but he reached out a hand to hold her where she was.

'Have I ever told you that you are a very beautiful woman?' he murmured huskily.

She felt herself blushing.

'Very beautiful and a pleasure to wake up to,' he continued, his lips curving in a half-smile.

'I've already said I will come in this morning to work for you,' she said in as light-hearted a tone as she could manage.

'So you have.' His smile deepened. 'I still think you are incredibly beautiful.' He reached out a hand to trace a gentle finger down the side of her face.

The feelings that light touch set up inside her were electric.

'You're not wearing a trace of make-up and your skin is fresh and smooth.' He sat up a little and the covers fell to his waist as he leaned a little closer to her. 'And do you know that your hair smells of camomile and honey?'

For a moment she thought he was going to kiss her. He leaned his head against the side of her face and gathered her silky hair up in his hands, caressing her scalp and tousling her hair in a seductive movement that made all her insides cry out for him.

'Marc, don't.' It was only a half-hearted protest as his hands moved to push down her dressing-gown so that it slipped from her shoulders.

'Don't?' He looked into her eyes and then feathered light kisses on her shoulders around the delicate shoe-string straps of her nightdress.

Her heart seemed to go wild, her pulses wildly pounding. When his large smooth hands pushed the straps down from her nightdress she made no protest. She leaned in against him, loving the gentle sweeping movement of his hands as they stroked down over her naked back.

He kissed the sides of her neck and then nibbled gently around her ear, his breath tickling the sensitive skin and making her laugh in a breathless way.

He pulled her down beside him and rolled over to look at her. 'Beautiful,' he murmured in a seductively husky tone. His eyes moved over her flushed face, her bright, shining eyes, and then down the long column of her neck towards the soft swell of her breasts.

He smiled and his head lowered towards her, his lips whispering along her neck, following the path downwards. She felt herself arch towards him, inviting his lips. When they touched her breast she felt herself losing complete control of any rational thought.

She was cocooned in a warm, hazy, sensual world where nothing mattered except here in Marc's arms.

'Sweetheart?' He leaned back on one elbow suddenly and looked down at her.

Marc was calling her sweetheart! She gazed up at him with a dreamy kind of wonder in her eyes. She did love him. She loved Marc Kingsley with all her heart. She reached up a hand and ran it softly up the strong planes of his face and into the thick darkness of his hair.

He seemed to grow very still at the inviting touch of her hand. She stopped, suddenly unsure. His gaze raked over her flushed skin framed by the tousled strawberry-blonde hair, then their eyes locked in a silent yet powerful communication.

She wanted this man; she wanted him with everything inside her, every grain of her soul, every beat of her heart.

When his head bent towards her again and his lips rained soft yet infinitely sensuous kisses over the satin-smooth contours of her face and his hands stroked down over the slender curves of her body, her heart was beating so wildly, it felt as if it was ready to explode.

'Darling Sabrina.' He murmured the words in a husky tone that just made her want to melt. 'Beautiful, delicious Sabrina.' As he spoke, his lips tasted her skin, moving lower and lower around her shoulders. They skipped almost playfully over her breasts and moved skilfully down over her abdomen in a whispering seduction that made her hands clench in sudden tight longing.

'Marc, please...' She was hardly aware of what she was saying; all her thoughts were centred on the mindblowing power of his caresses. 'Marc, I...' In that wild, abandoned moment she wanted to tell him that she loved him, but he moved and his lips met hers forcefully, cutting off any more coherent words.

The full length of his body pressed against hers now. He was heavy yet she welcomed that weight; she wanted him even closer. She felt as if she could never get close enough; she felt as if she wanted to merge into him, become part of him.

It was a moment before either of them became conscious of the sound of the phone ringing beside them. Marc pulled back from her and she sighed, reaching blindly for him. He glanced from her to the phone which was ringing insistently beside them on the bedside table. Then with an impatient movement he picked it up.

'Yes?'

To Sabrina his voice seemed to be coming from a long distance away. Her heart was pounding mercilessly. She had never felt so aroused, and the force of her feelings startled her... frightened her.

'Really?'

Dimly she was aware of a change in him as he sat up now. 'I see...that's good news. Yes, I'm on my way.'

As he put down the receiver and glanced at her she sensed rather than saw the dilemma in his expression.

'I'm sorry, honey, but I've got to go.' His voice was gentle, the dark eyes reassuringly soft on her flushed face. Yet the words had an immediate chilling effect on her senses.

What was she doing? Had she lost her mind completely? She reached frantically for her dressing-gown, which was tangled low down around her waist.

His hands stopped her. 'Don't look at me like that, Sabrina.'

'Like what?' Her voice held a sharp note. 'You are right, we must stop. I don't know what I'm doing. We are making a terrible mistake——'

'Sabrina.' His voice was firm as he cut across her.

She pulled away from him. She didn't want to listen to what he was going to say. 'You have an important business meeting at nine,' she said in a shaking voice.

'To hell with the meeting.' He put a hand on her shoulder but she shied away from him, sitting up abruptly and covering herself up with hands that couldn't move as fast as she wanted them to.

'Sabrina——'

'No.' She pressed her hands over her ears like a child frightened of hearing the truth. 'Don't say anything, Marc. Let's pretend this didn't happen.'

She got to her feet and without glancing at him again left the room.

As soon as she got back into her own bedroom she wanted to cry. Her whole body was trembling with reaction. That should never have happened. For heaven's sake, Marc didn't even like her, never mind love her. He had probably spent last night with Imogen Müller. That thought twisted and tormented inside her. She had made a complete fool of herself this morning; she had invited his caresses, luxuriated in his kisses. She despised herself for her weakness.

She headed straight for the shower, standing under the full force of its jet as if to wash away the memory of his hands against her body. But it lingered as she stepped out and dressed in a pale buttercup-yellow dress. It lingered as she dried her hair with violent haste. It teased and tormented her as she glanced at her reflection in the mirror.

Her cheeks were filled with tell-tale hectic colour, her eyes glimmered with an over-bright sparkle, her lips felt tender and even a little swollen from the intense kisses. She turned away and towards the door of her room, only to stop still before opening it.

She didn't think she could look Marc Kingsley in the face. She felt such a fool, felt that he would know now that her heart was heavily involved with him, her emotions tangled with a fierce desire for his love. Her hand lingered on the door-handle and she took deep, steadying breaths. She was just going to have to brazen this out. She would pretend that the episode had never happened. She wasn't going to make a laughing-stock of herself for anybody, least of all Marc Kingsley. With her head held high she walked into the hall.

He was waiting for her in the lounge.

Try as she did, she couldn't meet his eyes as she walked in. 'We had better leave,' she said briskly. 'You're going to be late.'

He didn't answer her straight away, just picked up his jacket and car keys. 'I've rung for my chauffeur to come and bring you into the office.'

'I see.' But she didn't see anything; she couldn't think straight no matter how hard she tried.

'You will have to re-schedule my meeting with Mr Hoffman when you get to the office. I've rung Anna and told her I won't be able to make the meeting, but she is not experienced enough to be able to handle the likes of Hoffman.'

Once more she was the reliable secretary. His brisk, efficient tones coming so soon after his passionate caresses made her cringe inside. Why was he rushing off like this? Why did she feel so empty, so bruised inside? 'Fine.' Her voice was airily light, as if she couldn't care less about anything.

'I'd appreciate it if you would smooth things out for me. Show Hoffman the contract that Anna typed up the other day for him.'

'Fine.' It was all she could say, in that terribly forced light-hearted tone. Her eyes collided with his and she felt like screaming at him for one wild moment.

The look on his face was grim, a million miles away from the way he had looked at her earlier. She turned abruptly away from him.

'See you later, then.'

When he walked out of the door she wanted to collapse in a heap on the floor and give in to the wild desire to sob. She bit down on the softness of her lips. She didn't care, she told herself frantically. Marc Kingsley could go to hell; she didn't care.

But she did care. She cared so deeply that she felt sore and her eyes hurt with the effort of not crying.

The chauffeur arrived to take her to the office. The journey seemed to pass in a haze. Sabrina felt so mixed up inside. Firstly she wanted Marc, then that need was replaced with a fierce anger. Marc didn't even like her. She had flung herself at him like a fool and he had been prepared to take advantage of her; there was nothing more to the episode than that.

Anna was scurrying around the office in a panic when she arrived. 'Mr Hoffman is here,' she hissed, making nodding motions through to the next office. 'I've told him that Mr Kingsley has been unavoidably detained and he nearly bit my head off.'

Sabrina nodded. 'It's all right, Anna, I'll deal with him,' she said calmly. 'Bring in the contract that you typed up for him yesterday.'

There was a look of immense relief in the other girl's eyes as she turned to do as she was asked.

Taking a deep breath, Sabrina strode into Marc's office as if she owned it. 'I'm very sorry you have been kept waiting, Mr Hoffman.'

The man was looking less than pleased. He was dressed in an expensive Armani suit, and gold cuff-links set with red rubies flashed with almost as much fire as his eyes as they moved over her slender figure then came to rest on her confident smile.

'I'm Mr Kingsley's personal assistant.' She gave herself a quick promotion, knowing that this man would not want to be fobbed off by a mere secretary.

He stood up and took her outstretched hand with a look on his face that suggested he was slightly pacified.

'Unfortunately Mr Kingsley has been detained on a very urgent matter that only he can deal with,' she continued in a brisk, no-nonsense tone. 'I'm sure you understand.' She put it in such a way that the other man found himself nodding in agreement.

'Sit down, please.' She waved him back into his chair and then with a flourish went and seated herself in Marc's chair behind the desk.

Lord alone knew what Marc would make of her sudden promotion and her audacity at sitting in his chair, but right at that moment she couldn't have cared less. He had told her to sort out Mr Hoffman and she intended to do the job properly.

Anna came in at that moment with the Hoffman file. She looked startled as she saw Sabrina sitting in Marc's chair.

'Thank you, Anna,' Sabrina said briskly as she held out her hand for the file. 'Would you get Mr Hoffman a coffee, please?'

Anna nodded and disappeared.

'Now, I have your contract here for you to look over.' Sabrina opened the file and ran her eyes efficiently over the contents. 'Here we are.' She took out the relevant document and passed it across to him. 'Perhaps you would like to look it over and then I will get Anna to make you another appointment to see Mr Kingsley?'

'Certainly.' The man smiled at her now, obviously pleased that he was going to get a glimpse of his contract.

She watched him reading it and prayed that he wouldn't ask her any awkward questions.

Anna brought in the man's coffee.

'Thank you, Anna.' Sabrina smiled at her. 'Could you also bring in the appointment book?'

Twenty minutes later Mr Hoffman left, looking satisfied and much more affable.

Sabrina heaved a sigh of relief as the door closed behind him. 'Thank heavens for that,' she muttered to Anna as she tidied away the Hoffman file.

'You did a good job of calming him down.' Anna grinned at her. 'I nearly dropped dead when I saw you sitting at Mr Kingsley's desk.'

Sabrina merely smiled. She didn't feel in a light-hearted mood.

'Where is Mr Kingsley, anyway?' Anna continued, undeterred by Sabrina's silence.

'No idea.' Sabrina didn't even want to think about that man, let alone talk about him.

But that was easier said than done. As the morning wore on and Sabrina settled into the typing that Marc had left her, his face kept floating into her mind.

Her skin burned when she thought about this morning. She had wanted Marc to make love to her so much, even though she had known that he had most probably spent the previous night with another woman. Her only defence was that she was in love with him. A weak excuse... but then she was weak when it came to Marc. He could wrap her around his little finger if he wanted to.

He arrived back over an hour later and she could feel her whole body burning as soon as he walked into the room and looked at her.

'Everything all right?' he asked immediately, his gaze raking over Sabrina in a most disconcerting way.

'Wonderful.' She couldn't help the sarcastic edge that came into her voice.

'Was Hoffman a problem?'

'No.'

Anna looked up and grinned. 'Well, he was a problem until Sabrina sorted him out.'

Marc nodded. 'Did you schedule another meeting?'

'Next Monday.' Anna was the one to answer. Sabrina was continuing with her typing, trying very much to ignore his presence.

'Good; get him on the phone for me, please.' He marched through to his office.

A little while later Marc's clipped voice came over the intercom. 'Sabrina, will you come in here a moment, please?'

Sabrina didn't move immediately. She didn't particularly want to go in and face him.

'Sabrina?' Anna looked over at her questioningly. 'Mr Kingsley is asking for you.'

'Yes, I heard.' Reluctantly she got to her feet and, running a smoothing hand over her hair, crossed the room to knock on his door.

He was deeply engrossed in some paperwork and barely glanced up as she came in.

'You asked for me?' She fixed her gaze on his hands rather than risk meeting his eyes.

'I believe you are now my personal assistant?' There was a glimmer of amusement in his tone that didn't escape Sabrina's notice.

'You asked me to smooth things over and I did.' Defensively she lifted her eyes to his and then promptly wished she hadn't. Those eyes had such an unnerving effect on her. It was like being drawn into a whirlpool of emotion—she felt as if she was drowning in that deep gaze.

'Don't be so quick to fly to the defensive,' he said calmly. 'I was just about to congratulate you. You did a good job. Mr Hoffman was impressed with you.'

For some reason his praise unnerved her even more. 'Thank you,' she said stiffly.

His eyes roved over her face and for a moment there was silence. 'Why don't we go and have lunch somewhere?'

The quietly asked question took her by surprise. 'I...I don't think so.'

'Why not?' He frowned heavily.

'Because...because I don't think it's a good idea,' she said, completely at a loss for any other reason that she could bear to tell him to his face.

'Well, I think it's a good idea.' He stood up. 'We need to talk.'

'Talk about what?' She followed him as he moved towards the door, a note of panic in her voice.

He didn't answer her, just opened the door and spoke briskly to Anna. 'I'm going out for lunch, Anna, so you will have to hold the fort for me.'

'All right.' Anna watched with interest as Marc picked up Sabrina's bag and handed it to her, then caught hold of her wrist and led her out of the office.

'Let go of me,' Sabrina spat as he led her along the corridor by a rather forcible grip.

He did, but only when they were in the lift on the way down to the underground car park.

She rubbed her wrist furiously. 'That hurt.'

'Sorry.' He didn't sound it. There was a kind of grim resolve in his manner. As if he had made up his mind about something.

The lift doors opened and he led the way towards his car.

'What on earth is this all about, Marc?' she asked, refusing to get into his car until he told her.

'I have a few things to say to you,' he replied calmly. She had the distinct impression that he was prepared to stand there all day waiting for her to get into the car if he needed to.

With a sigh she complied and slid into the comfortable seat. He got into the driver's seat, started the engine and drove out into the stream of traffic without saying another word.

'Where are we going?' She glanced across at his stern profile with apprehension.

'Wait and see,' came the irritating reply.

Sabrina pulled a face as she watched the London streets pass by in a busy blur of colours. So much for talking! He wouldn't even tell her where they were going.

In the event he took her to a very stylish restaurant in Richmond that backed out on to the River Thames.

He had no problem getting one of the best tables in a quiet, secluded corner with views out across the cold blueness of the river.

Why was she here? she asked herself as she glanced across and met Marc's eyes.

'Would you like a drink, Sabrina?' he asked solicitously as the waiter came over to take their order.

'White wine, please.' As soon as the waiter left them she leaned across towards him a little. 'I don't wish to sound ungrateful, Marc, but I had other plans for this afternoon.' It was a lie, but at that moment she would have done anything to save her pride. She couldn't bear for him to realise what she felt for him. How he would laugh at her.

He stared at her across the table. 'This is important.'

To whom? she wondered.

'I want you to reconsider coming to live in Paris,' he said starkly.

To say that Sabrina was knocked sideways by that statement was putting it mildly. She could only stare at him, her blue eyes wide and very, very puzzled.

'Why...why are you asking me that now?' Her voice shook slightly as she tried desperately to keep her emotions under cool control.

'Why not?' He smiled, but it was the smile of the predator. 'I want you, Sabrina,' he said in a firm, determined voice.

CHAPTER NINE

'HAVE you lost your senses?' She finally managed to find her voice.

'On the contrary,' he said calmly. 'I think my senses are in perfect working order.'

The waiter brought their drinks and asked if they were ready to order. 'Yes, I'll have the salmon.' Marc's voice was decisive although he hadn't even bothered to look at the menu.

'I'll have the same.' Sabrina would have asked for anything just to get rid of him so that she could continue with the conversation.

'It makes sense, Sabrina,' he said as soon as they were alone. 'We are good together.'

What did he mean by that? she wondered. 'Do you mean I'm a valuable secretary?' she asked in a voice that was low and strained.

'You are, yes, but obviously that's not why I'm asking you to come and live with me.' He sounded amused.

For a moment she was so bemused that she could only stare at him. 'You...you want me to live with you?' Her voice was a low, tremulous whisper.

'Of course.' The dark eyes were firm. 'I want you in my life, Sabrina.'

She fell silent. He looked so confident, as if he had no real doubts about her answer. She frowned.

'I can offer you a lot. I have a nice house just outside London, a villa in Portugal as well as my home in Paris.

I can give you a good lifestyle. Accounts in the top fashion houses, a new car, anything you want.'

Sabrina's eyes moved over his rugged features. It sounded as if he was trying to buy her! What about love? she wanted to ask. Or didn't that count for anything in his sophisticated, high-flying world?

For a moment she thought about Paris…when he had made her a similar offer. Back then she had naïvely believed it was because he felt something for her. She was under no such illusion now. Marc had made his opinion of her very clear.

'This may sound strange to you, Marc, but I don't particularly care if I live in a mansion or if I have a villa in Portugal or an apartment here in London. And I can afford to buy my own clothes, thank you.' Her voice was bitterly angry. 'Do you really think that I'm so cheap that you can buy me like that?'

He watched the angry expression on her face with a carefully bland expression. Strangely he didn't look angry at her outburst. 'I don't think that at all. I think you are a very beautiful, very intelligent woman,' he said quietly.

'So why are you asking me to come and live with you?'

'I've just told you.' His voice was coolly patient. 'You're beautiful and intelligent.'

'So is Imogen Müller,' she snapped briskly.

One dark eyebrow rose. 'Whatever made you ask about her?'

Sabrina glared at him. 'Because you are still having an affair with her.'

For just a moment the expression in his eyes lightened. 'Why, Sabrina…I do believe you are jealous,' he drawled with a smile.

Immediately she was filled with anger. 'Don't be so ridiculous . . . I couldn't care less who you see.' Her voice was bitterly earnest as she strove to convince him. Her pride seemed to be very much on the line and if she lost that she would be left with no defence . . . nothing.

'Anyway, as you pointed out this morning, it's none of my business.'

'This morning?' He looked puzzled for a moment, then he smiled. 'Oh, I see. You thought I was with Imogen last night.' He looked pleased at that idea for some reason. 'So you were jealous.'

'No, I was not jealous,' she stormed. 'Will you stop saying that? I couldn't care less.'

'You looked furious,' he said calmly. 'You looked as if you cared.'

'Well, looks can be very deceiving,' she said stonily. 'I was worried that something had happened to Garth.'

'Yes, Garth.' For a moment he frowned. 'All conversations seem to lead back to him.'

'That's because he is the only reason we are together.'

He didn't say anything to that. 'So will you come and live with me?' he asked again.

'No.' She didn't even have to think about her answer. She loved Marc very much but she couldn't live with a man who didn't love her, and he didn't love her. She knew that much for certain even though she couldn't really fathom out why he was suddenly asking her to live with him now . . . after everything he had said to her . . . all the insults.

'I see.' His eyes moved gently over the delicate curves of her face, the large, glimmering blue eyes. 'Do you mind me asking why not?'

'Yes, I mind.' She was damned if she was going to make a fool of herself by telling him that she was in love with him. That would really amuse him.

Their meals arrived. Sabrina stared down at the beautifully presented food and knew she couldn't eat a mouthful. Her throat felt dry and choked. She felt terribly upset. Why was Marc tormenting her like this?

He didn't touch his food either but reached for his glass. 'You once told me that you loved Garth. Did you mean that?'

The question threw her. If she answered it truthfully he wouldn't understand and she couldn't lie, not about that.

He took her silence as an affirmative answer. 'I see.' There was a long silence for a moment. 'Then I suppose I should tell you that Garth regained consciousness early this morning and he's going to be all right.'

For a moment all she could do was stare at him. Her relief was immense, and her heart thudded wildly and blissfully.

'I was at the hospital all last night because there were encouraging signs that he was coming out of the coma,' Marc continued in a brisk tone. 'The phone call this morning confirmed it.'

'Is that where you went this morning?' she asked breathlessly.

He nodded. 'Garth is still very weak and he couldn't talk much, but the doctors assured me he is on the road to recovery.'

'Oh.' She stared at him and her eyes brimmed over with tears all of a sudden. With the relief of Garth's recovery came the realisation of why Marc was suddenly asking her to come and live with him.

Now that Garth was getting better he was concerned that she was going to make problems in his mother's marriage. He was willing to put up with her for a while to get her off the scene.

Before she had even thought about what she was doing she was pushing her chair back from the table. 'When were you going to tell me?' she demanded angrily. 'After I had accepted your overly generous offer to become your mistress...your kept woman?' She rose to her feet, her eyes shimmering with hurt and with fury. 'Go to hell, Marc Kingsley.' Picking up her coat, she rushed from the restaurant before he could say a word. She wasn't aware of the startled looks she received from people dining at nearby tables or the waiters or the expression on Marc's face. All she could think of was getting out of there.

It was raining outside but she hardly noticed as she rushed down the crowded streets in search of a taxi. Tears were streaming down her face but she wasn't really aware of them. Her mind was filled with Marc. He had known when he came home this morning that Garth's condition was improving, and he had said nothing. His one thought must have been to prevent her from going anywhere near Garth.

She remembered how he had kissed her. Marc Kingsley was very good at the art of seduction. Had it been in his mind while he was caressing her and telling her how beautiful she was that he could entice her away from Garth? It seemed very likely.

Marc must have been racking his brains all morning on a plan to lure her away from his stepfather. She could hardly believe that he had the arrogant gall to ask her to become his mistress!

How little he must respect her. He thought she was pretty; he thought she was a good secretary. He had weighed the odds and thought why not take her on for a couple of years, or maybe a couple of months? Just until Garth lost interest, of course. He thought of her as an object, nothing more, an object to be bought. Wasn't it George Bernard Shaw who said, 'If you can't get rid of the family skeleton, you may as well make it dance'?

She held up a hand to a taxi but it didn't stop. She was getting completely drenched now. The coat she was wearing was not really suitable for such a downpour.

She was aware of a car drawing level with her at the pavement and glanced around. She was horrified to see it was Marc.

He wound down the electric window. 'Get in, for heaven's sake,' he said briskly. 'You're getting soaked.'

'I wouldn't get in if my life depended on it,' she told him furiously.

'You are being ridiculous,' he ground out. 'Now get in before I come and carry you in.'

'I've told you, get lost.' Another taxi was passing and she put up her hand in desperation. She could hardly believe her good fortune when it stopped.

She climbed in, glancing nervously behind her as if Marc Kingsley was going to appear suddenly and get in the cab with her. She was relieved to see his car pulling away from them.

'Where to, miss?' the taxi driver asked abruptly.

She gave her address and leaned back. Her mind whirled in circles on that journey. All she could think of was Marc's audacity. She closed her eyes.

Now that she knew Garth was all right she felt exhausted, as if all the nights when she had lost sleep had suddenly caught up with her at once. She could hardly think straight any more.

When the vehicle pulled up outside her apartment she opened her eyes and sat forward to ask how much she owed. When he told her she looked for her bag. It was only then that she realised that she had left it in the restaurant.

The taxi driver repeated the amount of money she owed him as she sat looking at him blankly. Her money was in her bag and she couldn't get into her apartment to get him any more because her keys were also in her bag.

'Look, miss, I haven't got all day.' The man was starting to sound irritated and she didn't really blame him.

The door opened and a familiar voice enquired lazily, 'How much does the lady owe you?'

Sabrina stared at Marc, her heart thudding. His face was impassive, his eyes darkly intense. The driver repeated the sum of money and Marc duly paid him, and gave him a handsome tip, if the profuse thanks of the man were anything to go by.

Reluctantly Sabrina stepped out of the taxi and watched it drive away.

'This is yours, I believe?' Marc asked her drily as he held out her black leather bag.

'Thank you.' She could say nothing else. She felt foolish in the extreme. She didn't dare look at him as she opened her bag to search for her keys.

He stood beside her silently watching and unnerving her completely. She found her keys and then fumbled with them so much that she dropped them.

He picked them up for her and opened the front door for her.

'Thanks.' She got her purse out and took out the money she owed him for the taxi.

'What's that?' he asked as she held it out to him. His voice held a note of anger now.

'For the taxi.'

'Don't be ridiculous.' He strode past her and into her apartment, leaving her standing on the doorstep with the money and no other choice but to follow him inside.

'Marc, I appreciate your bringing my bag for me,' she said frostily, 'but I don't want you here. I've taken just about all the insults I'm going to take from you.'

'I have no intention of insulting you.' He leaned back against the staircase looking relaxed and at perfect ease, yet she had the strange feeling that underneath that surface was a watchful, cautious man. 'Anyway, don't you think that you at least owe me a cup of coffee for bringing your bag?'

'Not really.' She took off her coat and caught sight of her reflection in the hall mirror. She looked ghastly. Her hair was wet and her eyes were streaked with tears.

'Perhaps I should make you one?' he said from behind her. 'Why don't you go and get changed?'

For a moment she was forcibly reminded of the first night she had met him and he had made her coffee. She had been so attracted to him... but even then she had been aware of how dangerous that feeling could be. She should have listened to those warning signals...she should never have got mixed up with this man.

She turned and glared at him.

'You're not going to lose your temper again, are you?' he asked before she could say anything. 'You've got one hell of a temper.'

'Do you really blame me?'

He pursed his lips. 'I thought you over-reacted a little.'

As she looked set to explode again he held up his hands. 'I didn't mean to upset you, Sabrina. I'm sorry.'

She stared at him. The awful thing was that now she felt like crying again.

'I guess I underestimated how much you feel for Garth. I kind of hoped...' He trailed off and shrugged. 'Well, it doesn't matter what I hoped. I just want to say that I don't really think you're that scheming mercenary woman that I accused you of being and, for what it's worth, I'm sorry.'

She had thought that she would have gloated when that apology came but strangely she couldn't revel in it. She didn't feel triumphant; she felt strangely numb.

'Was it some sort of test, offering me your house and your villa and your money?' she asked him in a dull tone.

He thought about that for a moment and then shrugged broad shoulders. 'Some sort of test...yes.' There was a strange husky sound to his voice, a sound that caught and played on her heart-strings.

She swallowed hard. 'You know I have no intention of taking Garth away from Nadine. We haven't got that kind of relationship.' She hesitated for a second, her mind running along what she could tell him. 'And I'm not after his money or his power.'

'You don't have to tell me anything, Sabrina.' He raked a hand through his dark hair impatiently. 'Look, I haven't got time for that coffee anyway. I should be getting back to the office.'

She nodded. 'I understand.'

'Do you?' He smiled but it held little humour.

For a moment she hesitated and then slowly she took off the engagement ring that he had bought for her. 'I think you had better have this back, Marc,' she said quietly. 'I can't go on with this charade.'

His face hardened; somewhere along his jaw a muscle pulsed beneath the skin.

'I don't want the damn thing back,' he grated harshly. 'Keep it as a souvenir.'

She bit down on the softness of her lip, willing herself not to cry. 'I can't keep it, Marc, I——'

'Then give it to some charity.' He wrenched open the door. 'Goodbye, Sabrina.'

It was only when he was gone that her air of indifference crumbled and she leant against the door and felt as if her heart would break.

CHAPTER TEN

THE field of daffodils moved in the spring sunshine as a sudden breeze whipped across the rugged countryside, swaying them back and forth like a golden sea. Sabrina put a hand up to push her hair away from her face and turned to walk back towards her hotel.

It was a beautiful day. The sunshine seemed to make the grass even greener against the sharp outline of the mountains. Daffodils were everywhere, along the edges of the roads, down by the lake, fluttering in a golden display that only the Lake District seemed to give on such a grand scale—perhaps due to William Wordsworth's poem?

Sabrina turned her thoughts towards that poem in an attempt to stop herself thinking about Marc. But, just like every day since she had last seen him, the image of his face seemed to haunt her.

It was nearly two weeks now since she had tried to give him back his ring. The first week she had spent walking around her apartment in a kind of daze. She had listened to the news reports that Garth was growing stronger, that his family were gathered around his bedside and were all overjoyed by his recovery, and although she had shared in their relief there was a sadness deep inside her.

Her father didn't need her; he had his own daughter Madeline, a stepson, a loving wife. She was an outsider and her very existence could cause untold problems for

Garth. She'd fought the desire to go and see him. Instead she'd packed a bag and taken the train up to Windermere.

She had needed desperately to get away from London. The Lake District had been a spur-of-the-moment decision. She had been looking through *The Times* to see if Marc had placed an advertisement announcing the end of their engagement, and her eye had been caught by the advertisement for the Lakes.

There had still been no announcement about the end of her engagement, but she felt it was just a matter of time. Marc was obviously trying to wait a little longer, maybe until Garth was out of hospital and back home with Nadine. Then he would probably deem it safer to make the announcement.

She stopped and leaned against a gate, her gaze sweeping down towards the cold blue water of Windermere. Some lambs were skipping across the fields, frolicking in the spring sunshine.

With a smile Sabrina turned and walked on. She did feel better up here. At least she was sleeping at night now, the long walks and the fresh air taking the pallor from her skin and giving her a healthy glow.

Her hotel was just visible now, nestling between the fields and the lake. A country inn rather than a hotel, it was warm and cosy inside, low-beamed with roaring log fires in all the rooms. Sabrina quickened her pace. It was downhill all the way from here and the thought of a hot coffee at the end of her walk spurred her on.

Although the courtyard at the side of the inn held a number of cars there was no one in the lounge when she walked in. Dusty, the resident golden retriever, was sleeping in front of the fire. He opened one eye as she walked in and then closed it wearily.

'Hello, anyone about?' Sabrina leaned against the bar as she craned her head to see if anyone was standing through the other side. There was no reply.

Dusty stood up and shook himself sleepily before wandering over to say hello to her.

'Well, at least you're pleased to see me.' Sabrina bent down and stroked his soft coat. 'How about coming for a walk with me tomorrow, Dusty? It gets kind of lonely out there for a city girl on her own.'

The dog yawned as if even the thought made him exhausted.

'Do you think I could tag along as well?'

The casually asked question coming from behind her made all her senses reel. It couldn't be! she thought hazily. It just couldn't! Perhaps she was imagining things.

She turned slowly and her eyes rested with a kind of hungry disbelief on Marc's rugged features. 'What on earth are you doing here?' she asked in amazement.

'I was going to ask you the same thing.' For a moment his eyes moved over her slender figure in her close-fitting black jeans and thick woollen jumper. 'You look fabulous,' he said huskily.

So did he, she thought with a catch of her breath as she looked at him. He was wearing casual clothing— blue jeans and a chunky blue and white jumper that did amazing things to an already perfect physique. 'Is this just a coincidence?' Her voice was barely a whisper. She didn't know what to think.

'No,' he whispered back. 'I came looking for you.'

She stared at him, her eyes wide. 'Why? Is there something wrong?' She swallowed hard. 'Is it Garth?'

'No. Garth is fine.' He moved nearer to her. Although his voice was relaxed and reassuring there was a tense look about him. His face looked drawn, as if he hadn't been sleeping properly.

'Are you sure?' Her voice trembled alarmingly as he stood close beside her.

'Of course I'm sure. I only saw him this morning.' He smiled at her. 'The doctors say he can come home soon.'

'That's wonderful.' She brushed a nervous hand through her hair. 'How did you know I was here, Marc?'

'I hope you don't mind but I used the key to your front door and after a little bit of searching I found *The Times* newspaper with the advertisement for here circled. It was the only lead I had on you, so in desperation I followed it up.'

She frowned. 'Marc, I've already told you that I won't make any trouble in Garth's life. You don't need to come running after me like this. I'm not a problem to him or to you.'

'Ah . . . but that's where you're wrong,' he said softly. 'You are a problem . . . a big, big problem.'

She glared at him and her eyes glimmered bright blue and incredibly large in the delicate face. 'I'm not, Marc . . . how many times do I have to tell you?'

'Garth wants to know why you haven't been in to see him.'

This softly asked question stopped her in her tracks.

'He's asking for me?' Her heart seemed to flutter for a moment with a cross between happiness and then depression.

'Of course he's asking for you.' Although the words were spoken briskly there was no hint of annoyance in them. He caught hold of her shoulders and then moved a hand to cup her chin so that she was forced to look up into the darkness of his eyes.

The touch of his hands made her skin burn.

'Why didn't you tell me, you little fool?' he grated softly.

'Tell you what?' She closed her eyes—she couldn't bear to look at him.

'Sabrina.' His voice held a hint of impatience. 'I know.'

Her eyes flew open at that.

'The laugh of the thing is that you are so damn like him. Now when I look at you I can see it.' His eyes moved carefully over her features.

'You know?' For a moment her mind went whirling chaotically. How did he know? Had he found something at her house?

'Garth told me,' Marc said gently as she saw the questions in her eyes.

Sabrina's relief was immense. It was like a huge cloud lifting from over the top of her. She bit down on her lip and suddenly wanted to cry.

'Why the hell didn't you tell me that Garth is your father?' he rasped suddenly. 'You let me go through hell.'

'I'm sorry.' She shook her head and desperately tried to gather her thoughts together. 'But I didn't know what to do. I had promised Garth. We had discussed it before his accident, and he was worried about the repercussions of telling Nadine... of the papers getting hold of the story.' A tear trickled down the smooth paleness of her cheek. 'I didn't dare say anything. I couldn't do that to him.'

He wiped away the tear with a gentle finger, making her tremble violently.

'I'm sorry if I upset you,' she said in a low voice.

'Oh, Sabrina,' he groaned. 'I should be apologising to you. I said some dreadful things. I was so furious.'

She looked away from him. 'Well, it was understandable. You thought I was breaking up your mother's marriage...'

'I have a confession to make...' Marc hesitated as he looked down at her. 'My reasons for being so furious were not entirely honourable.'

She looked up at him in utter confusion now. 'What do you mean?'

For a moment he hesitated. 'Why don't we go somewhere more comfortable and discuss this?'

She glanced at one of the settees at the far side of the room.

'I was thinking of somewhere with a little more privacy,' he said, following her gaze.

She looked back into his eyes and her heart missed a beat with a violent skip. 'I...I don't think so, Marc.' The truth of the matter was that she was frightened of being anywhere too secluded with him...afraid that her emotions might run away with her, that she would end up making a fool of herself.

'It was nice of you to come up here and tell me about Garth and I appreciate——'

He pulled her almost roughly into his arms, cutting her stiffly polite little speech off in mid-sentence.

'I don't want your thanks, Sabrina, I want to talk things through with you. There are things I need to say.'

'Please, Marc.' She looked away from his disconcerting eyes, frightened in case he saw too much in her expression. She realised that he was probably just feeling guilty now that he knew the truth...that he was only here to say he was sorry, but she didn't want his apologies. She couldn't bear for him to be kind to her in case she broke down and said something she really would regret.

'Please... let go of me. We have nothing to say.'

'I'm not going,' he said firmly. 'I realise you are angry with me... you have every right, but I can't leave things the way they are. It's driving me crazy.' His voice was urgent and held a husky edge that did incredible things to Sabrina's heart-rate.

'Let's go up to your room and talk,' he murmured persuasively. 'Please, Sabrina.'

'Don't do this to me, Marc... I can't bear it,' she said in a low, trembling voice.

'Just ten... fifteen minutes of your time and then if you want I will go,' he said levelly. 'I promise, Sabrina... I won't outstay my welcome.'

She hesitated and then found herself nodding.

The sound of someone clearing her throat discreetly made them break apart just a little.

Mrs Roberts, the owner of the hotel, stood behind the bar with a beaming smile on her face. 'Did I hear someone calling for a drink?'

'You certainly did.' Marc was quick to regain his composure and gave her one of his most dazzling smiles. 'We'll have a bottle of your best champagne and two glasses.'

A chilled bottle of Dom Pérignon was placed before them. Marc paid her and then picked it up with the delicate crystal glasses. 'I think we will retire with this to somewhere more private,' he said openly.

Sabrina felt herself colouring with embarrassment as the woman smiled at her.

'I...I don't know why you said that,' she said in a low tone as Marc led the way out of the room. 'She has probably got completely the wrong idea now.'

'Do you think so?' For a moment there was a gleam in Marc's eye that made her breath catch.

She followed him upstairs with a feeling of deep foreboding...this was a mistake. She needed to keep her distance from this man. He was capable of turning her into a gibbering wreck...of stripping her of any small vestige of pride that she had left.

He stopped at the top of the stairs. 'Which one is your room?'

'End of the corridor.' Sabrina's hand trembled slightly as she took out her room key. She still couldn't believe that this was happening. She had dreamt on a few occasions that Marc would apologise to her for the awful accusations he had made, but now she didn't want his contrition...she wanted much more from Marc, more than he could ever give. She swallowed on a hard knot in her throat. She was going to have to be very brave...accept Marc's apologies gracefully and hope that he didn't guess at her true feelings.

A fire burnt brightly in the grate, flickering shadows over the pretty room with its fresh primrose-yellow walls and the huge double bed with cool linen sheets turned back so invitingly.

The champagne cork flew off with a loud bang and Marc filled the two glasses and handed her one.

'Does Garth know that you are here with me?' she asked him in a small uncertain voice.

'Yes, Garth knows.' Marc smiled at her. 'I've told him all about us.'

Sabrina had to swallow hard again. 'You mean you told him all about our sham of an engagement,' she said in a low voice that only barely disguised the hurt she was feeling.

'I told him everything.' Marc watched her with a speculative look in his dark eyes.

Sabrina sipped her champagne and for a moment she remembered that day in Paris when she had sipped champagne and fallen very much under Marc Kingsley's spell.

'Anyway,' she continued dully, 'at least you will be free to carry on your relationship with Imogen Müller now. She was obviously very upset about our phoney engagement.'

'I have no interest in carrying on my relationship with Imogen Müller,' he said firmly.

'Oh!' Her eyes flew to his. It was ridiculous how pleased she was to hear that... as if it made any difference.

'I'm only interested in carrying on a relationship with you,' he said quietly.

For just a second hope soared inside her. Then she squashed it before it got out of hand. He was being kind. 'Next you're going to be telling me that you think of me as your other sister,' she said bitterly.

'No... I wouldn't dream of telling you anything so absurd,' he said crisply. He put down his champagne and raked a hand through his hair. 'I've made such a mess of everything...' he said hoarsely. 'I... I was so suspicious... so intensely jealous.'

'Jealous?' She looked at him with a frown. 'Jealous of what?'

'Of you and Garth, of course.' He shook his head. 'You've no idea what it's been doing to me, Sabrina... I've been out of my mind with it.'

'You were jealous...' For a moment she couldn't comprehend that.

'I told you my motives for being so angry weren't exactly honourable,' he said with a shrug. 'Oh, at the beginning before I met you I was furious when I thought Garth was having an affair... I was determined to put a stop to it. Then I met you and——' he hesitated '—I looked into your blue eyes and I felt an overwhelming attraction to you.'

Sabrina swallowed hard. 'Marc... you don't need to make excuses, you know. I hold no grudges about your behaviour; I——'

'Hell, Sabrina, surely you know me well enough by now to realise I'm not trying to excuse my anger... I'm telling you how I felt, for heaven's sake!'

The intense emotion in his voice startled her almost as much as his words. She hardly dared to believe what he was saying to her. She just stood there staring wordlessly at him.

'I saw you at that restaurant having dinner with Garth and I thought you were the most beautiful woman I had ever met. When you turned those deep blue eyes up at me and smiled, it blew my mind.' His voice was a husky rasping sound in the silence. 'I desperately wanted you and yet you refused to have anything to do with me.' For a moment his lips twisted into a semblance of a grim smile. 'No one had ever refused a date with me so flatly before.'

For a brief moment Sabrina's lips curved at the arrogant statement. Marc wasn't bragging, he was just stating a fact. A fact that triggered an alarm bell deep inside her. She hardly dared to believe that this wonderful, handsome man whom she loved with all her heart really was so infatuated with her. Was it more the case that he was interested because she had been out of his reach?

'When you turned down my offer of a job in Paris I was livid...eaten away with jealousy that the one woman I wanted more than anything or anybody else wanted Garth.'

'Oh, Marc.' Her voice was a mere whisper. 'I...I can hardly take all of this in. I thought you hated me.' A tear trickled down the smoothness of her cheek. She wanted so much to believe that he really cared for her but she was so afraid of being hurt. 'Please don't say it if you don't mean it...I couldn't bear it.'

He moved across to her and put his hands on her shoulders. 'I mean it more than I've ever meant anything,' he said huskily.

The touch of his hands against her shoulders seemed to burn right through her. She looked up into his eyes. He took her champagne glass and put it down next to his. The next moment he was cradling her close against him. She could smell the familiar aroma of his cologne, hear the rapid thud of his heart that seemed to match hers exactly.

'Please believe me, Sabrina...I'm crazy about you.' His lips roved over the pale softness of her cheeks and then found the sweetness of her lips.

For a while she surrendered to the torrent of emotions inside her as she responded to that kiss. It was so bittersweet. She could feel her whole body trembling with reaction. Her knees felt like buckling under her, and she clung to him weakly. And at the same time she was crying openly... tears were streaming down her face.

'Darling... please don't cry,' he murmured thickly. 'I can't bear to upset you again.'

Desperately she strove to pull herself together. 'I'm sorry...I'm really sorry.' She pulled away from him with great difficulty. She was behaving foolishly. All right, so Marc had said he was crazy about her... but did he really mean it? Marc was a man with a reputation for breaking hearts. Was he just playing a game with her emotions? Was he only interested in her because she had turned him down once? All kinds of insecure thoughts raced through her as she looked up at him with wide, vulnerable eyes.

She couldn't believe that Marc Kingsley was serious about her... it just seemed too good to be true.

'I don't want to hurt you, Sabrina...I just want to know if there is any chance for us to start again.'

'I...I don't know, Marc.' She turned away from him. She couldn't think clearly when she looked into those dark eyes.

There was a moment's silence in the room. A moment when tension seemed to fill the air so thickly that you could almost hear it in the ticking of the clock, the beating of her heart. 'I don't know what you mean when you say start again...I'm so frightened,' she admitted on a husky whisper.

He moved to stand behind her. He was very close but he didn't touch her—it was as if he was holding himself back.

'When I took you out for lunch on that last day in London and asked you to come and live with me I really meant it, Sabrina.'

She didn't turn around...her mind was trying to make some rational sense. She wanted to think clearly without her emotions clouding her judgement, but that seemed almost impossible.

'Oh, I know I made a mess of it...it sounded more like a business proposal than I intended.' He hesitated. 'But I have my pride as well, Sabrina. I wasn't sure what reaction I would receive...I was hedging my bets—offering you everything in case my love wasn't enough. When you turned me down I thought it was because you were in love with Garth.'

She turned to look at him then. 'Your love?' Her voice trembled alarmingly but somehow she managed to look upwards into his eyes.

'Oh, yes...' he whispered. 'I love you, Sabrina...have since I first set eyes on you.'

'Oh, Marc.' She stretched her arms up and around his neck, pressing her body close to his...so close that she wanted just to melt into him. She didn't want to think any more...she just wanted to feel.

He held her tightly, then suddenly he swung her off her feet and carried her to the chair by the fire so that she was sitting on his knee.

'Lord, you don't know how often I've dreamt of you putting your arms around me like that.' His voice tickled against her ear as he kissed the side of her neck, then across her cheek to find her mouth in a hungry, intense kiss that took her breath completely away.

She clung to him, kissing him back with just as much hunger.

His hands moved to slide down her body and she was filled with wild desire. When his fingers started to unfasten the top of her jumper she made no move to stop him. She wanted to feel his hands against her skin...had dreamt of it in her wildest dreams.

He started to pull her top up, then hesitated as their eyes met. 'I'm rushing things, aren't I?' he asked with a lop-sided grin that tugged at her heart-strings more than anything else.

'I...' She shrugged, self-conscious for a moment.

'I'm sorry, darling,' he said in a low tone, reaching up to stroke her hair away from her face so that he could see her clearly. 'You'll have to forgive me if I seem impatient...but I've yearned for you for so long.'

For a while they just stared into each other's eyes.

Sabrina took a deep shuddering breath. 'I...I find it hard to believe that you've yearned for me, Marc,' she said in a hushed, trembling voice. 'Not when there have been so many beautiful women in your life.' It was strange, but she still felt this deep insecurity, this almost painful jealousy when she thought of the other women in Marc's life.

He smiled tenderly. 'No one has ever stirred me up with such fierce intensity before,' he said gently.

'Is it...is it because you thought you couldn't have me?' She couldn't meet his eyes as she asked that question. But she had to ask it. She had to know how he felt...what her chances were that he was serious.

He didn't answer her immediately and she felt her breath catch painfully.

'No one has ever kept me awake at nights...no one has ever haunted my every waking thought.' He shook his head. 'And I've never felt the urge to propose to anyone before.'

For just a second her heart faltered. He was teasing of course, she thought as her eyes darted back to him.

'Just...just what are you proposing?' she asked unsteadily.

'Well...before I say——' he darted a quick glance at the bed behind her '—how about telling me if I'm making a complete fool of myself here?' he asked with a raised eyebrow. 'Is there any chance that you might have some feelings for me?'

Although the words were asked lightly, the eyes that held hers were very serious.

She hesitated and then some imp of mischief made her want to tease him back. 'Maybe some...small chance.'

For a moment he frowned, then as their eyes met his darkened. 'I do believe you're getting your own back here—tormenting me.' With each word he kissed her.

Then swiftly, unexpectedly, her jumper was expertly discarded and she was sitting in just a lacy bra.

'Now,' he whispered against her ear, 'where was I?' He proceeded to kiss her face then move down her neck, his hands smoothing over her silky skin like bands of fire against her delicate senses.

When his lips found hers again she was almost incoherent with desire. She certainly didn't have any resources of strength to tease him further.

'Now tell me that you have some feelings for me,' he demanded in a husky drawl.

She looked up at him, at the darkness of his eyes and skin, the white smile, the sensuous lips, and her heart seemed to turn over. 'You...you know I do,' she whispered softly. 'I...love you, Marc.'

His eyes seemed to darken to deepest black as she said those words.

'I've tried so hard to fight it,' she continued in a low tone. 'Even now I'm . . . I'm terrified that this isn't going to work. That you are just playing with me. That I'm going to be very hurt.'

'I'd never hurt you, Sabrina . . .' He said the words almost fiercely. 'I mean to hold you and protect you from being hurt ever again.'

'Oh, Marc . . .' She was half laughing, half crying. 'If only . . .' She trailed off as a sudden thought struck her. 'What about Nadine and Madeline? Do they know the truth about me?'

'Darling Sabrina. Garth told all of us about you and he told us before I had a chance to say anything to him.'

'How did they take it?' She asked the question breathlessly.

'They were startled . . . shocked, I suppose, as I was.' He kissed the side of her face. 'But they don't think any less of Garth and they certainly don't think any less of you. They are looking forward to seeing you again.'

'Oh, Marc.' Sabrina buried her head in against his chest, breathing in the tangy aroma of his cologne in a relieved and blissful way. 'I just couldn't bear to upset them.'

He kissed the top of her head and then lifted her face so that his lips found hers. It was a few moments before they spoke again. Then, 'My darling girl,' he murmured in a husky voice against her ear. 'You are Garth's daughter and I hope and pray that you will consent and become Nadine's daughter-in-law.'

'Marc!' Sabrina sat up very straight and looked down at him. 'So you do mean it . . .'

'I have never been more serious. I love you with all my heart, Sabrina, and I would be the happiest man on earth if you would become my wife.'

Sabrina could only see his handsome features through a hazy blur of tears for a moment. 'I hardly dare to believe it,' she said in a low voice. 'I thought you were in love with Imogen Müller... I thought——'

'Oh, Sabrina.' He shook his head. 'Please believe me, I'm not in love with Imogen Müller. I was never serious about her. In fact I had finished our relationship before I met you. She only came to my office the other day because she said her father had sent her... that she was there to discuss business. I soon found out that wasn't the case. Her father told me in no uncertain way that she had no authorisation to discuss his business.'

'Oh!' She smiled and for a second her lips curved in a bright smile of sheer happiness. That was before Marc had claimed them in a fiercely passionate kiss. His hands moved over her body and she arched against him, loving him, wanting him more than she had ever thought possible.

'My darling Sabrina... please, please put me out of my misery and say yes,' he murmured huskily against the heat of her skin.

She smiled and her hand reached upwards to stroke through the vibrant thickness of his hair. 'Marc Kingsley, I love you with all my heart and I would marry you tonight if I could.'

It was a long time before either of them spoke again, and then Marc whispered seductively against her ear, 'I'll get a special licence but I doubt very much if we could get married tonight. In the meantime, would you be very scandalised if I suggested moving to that double bed?'

HARLEQUIN PRESENTS®

Coming soon...

June 1997—Long Night's Loving (#1887)

by Anne Mather

New York Times bestselling author,
with over 60 million books in print

"Pleasure for her readers." —*Romantic Times*

and

July 1997—A Haunting Obsession (#1893)

by Miranda Lee

one of Presents' brightest stars,
with over 10 million books sold worldwide

"Superb storytelling." —*Romantic Times*

Top author treats from Harlequin Presents.
Make this summer the hottest ever!